GREGORY EL HARVEY

FACES

IN

THE SHADOWS

A NOVEL

Books by Gregory El Harvey

JACKSONVILLE

Autobiographical
FACES IN THE SHADOWS

Serial
THE PATTERN OF A SNOWFLAKE
DRAGONS MORE DECENT THAN MEN
DRAGONS IN LOVE
TO DIE IN THE COLDEST WINTER
THE AUTONOMOUS ASSASSINS

Cover painting: *Faces and Signs* by Gregory El Harvey
(www.gregharveygallery.com)

To my daughter Myanna,
who read the manuscript
and understood why I wrote it,
and to the dog Thor,
who in good faith took his place
as my protector.

ACKNOWLEDGMENT

I am grateful to my daughter Cassia for her help
with the publication process.

RONI

Chapter 1

I first saw her as she entered the waiting room in Neurology and then walked toward me. I guessed that her hair, which had been pulled flat and tightly ponytailed, was brown.

"Hi. Mr. Le Haley? I'm Dr. Feinman," she said with a half smile, offering her hand.

"Hi, Dr. Feinman," I answered, shaking the hand as I rose from my chair.

She led me to an examination room, shifted a chair perfunctorily for me to sit in, and closed the door. She sat, but did not pull herself close to the desk. She looked at me for just a second, then reached forward, opened the folder of my records, and said calmly, "So, how have you been? How do you feel?"

I watched as she crossed her legs and then adjusted her lab coat, which was unbuttoned. Her dress seemed to be pink. I was fascinated by the

1

constancy of the severe yet benign expression on her face. Her eyes seemed to be green . . . I wanted them to be green . . . yes, I was certain they were green, very green. Although I was glad she was not wearing glasses, I couldn't resist picturing her with wire-rims. But realizing that they would hide her wonderful eyes and neutralize her severe expression, I took them away. Looking at her round intelligent head, I replied, "I'm okay. I'm fine, thanks." Her smile at this was somehow what I needed, and I felt myself relax. I watched her fingers as she turned the pages of my folder.

"Yes?"

"Well, a little tired. Maybe it's age. It's just the fatigue, I think."

She nodded. "I think so, yes. You're only in your late fifties. That's pretty young. I mean, these days that's very young. People are living past a hundred all the time. So, it has to be the fatigue. It's one of the major complaints patients with MS have."

"It's not too bad."

"Good, that's good. You know, I keep wanting to put an *e* in your name. It's an interesting spelling."

"Yes. My parents wanted to make a distinction of some kind. I'm not really sure what the point was. But no . . . no *e*, I'm afraid. It's just Stanly."

Leaning back in her chair, as if to avoid looking at my name in print, she asked, "Any other problems?"

"No. I think I'm okay."

After a moment she said, "You know, your Evoked Potential results show you're not getting much to the back of the brain. Even the right eye came back as zero. Since the left is NLP, at this point you just aren't seeing much. Still nothing in the left."

I shook my head. "It's not coming back."

"No. I think not. I don't want to sound negative, but it's been too long. You're seeing a little in the right, but all the fields are either gone or corrupted. You should be really careful about stairs and crossing the street."

"I've been looking into Braille."

"That's probably a good idea. You're at least legally blind. I mean, you've been declared. Did they give you a letter?"

"Yes."

She nodded, glancing at a page in the folder. "Uh, yeah, I see that. And so, what about the Braille, how far have you gone with it?"

"Well, actually, I'll probably not do it. Maybe if I was younger. I think, for me, technology is probably the way to go. You know, electronic readers, things like that. I don't know."

"Whichever way you go, preparation is certainly wise. How about the injections? Are you okay with them?"

"They're not a problem."

"That's good. People hate them. And, side effects okay?"

I shrugged. "Not too bad."

"They're supposed to diminish over time."

"I know," I replied. "They haven't diminished. I'd say they're about the same as when I started. But it doesn't bother me, considering the alternative."

"Yeah, you were pretty sick when you came into the hospital the first time. I was reading through your folder. You were here, like, eight days, right?"

"Yes."

"But anyway, that's good. A lot of people can't tolerate interferon. Just keep taking it."

I nodded.

"And the immunomodulator?" she asked. "Any side effects?"

"No. Everything's okay with that too."

"How's work going?"

I lifted my shoulders again. "They're very understanding at work. It's a good situation. Very nice people. I use magnifiers to do the work."

"They're okay when you take sick days?"

"Oh, yeah. They're very understanding."

She sighed. "Okay, well, you can expect more fatigue. How's the numbness?"

"Still the same."

"Which side is it, the right?"

"Yes. Almost the whole right side. And other places."

After a moment she said, "Just take it one day at a time, okay?"

"Yes, right."

"Okay," she said, pushing her chair back, "why don't you get up on the table and we'll take a look at your optic nerves and check your muscle strength."

Following the examination she accompanied me in silence to the front desk, where she again presented her hand to me, along with another smile. Then she simply walked away, as if pressed by many demands. After handing my papers to the receptionist, I turned to see the lab coat of Dr. Feinman disappear through a doorway.

It was about a week later that she phoned me at home. "Hi, Mr. Le Haley?"

"Yes. Hi, Dr. Feinman."

"Oh, you've got caller ID."

"No, I just recognized your voice."

"Oh. Well, I have good news that your labs came back okay. Liver enzymes, everything. Everything was okay."

"Good, that's great to hear. Thanks. And thanks for calling and following up and everything."

"Oh sure, it's not a problem."

"You must be really busy. It's always busy there. At least, it seems that way to me. So, thanks."

"That's okay. No, I had just gotten home and had a few minutes. So, how do you feel, how is the vision? Or any other changes?"

"I'm okay," I answered. "The vision seems to be holding fairly steady. I think I sort of unconsciously monitor it."

"That's perfect. Don't focus on it, but be ready to pick up on any change."

For some reason, I became conscious of enjoying her voice. I said clumsily, "I will. Okay."

"Right. Good. Keep watch on things. Call me, whenever. It's okay, they'll find me."

"Yes, thanks, I will."

"Okay. Well, take care of yourself, Mr. Le Haley."

"Yes, I will, Dr. Feinman. Thanks."

"Well, we'll see you."

"Yes," I said. "And thanks again for calling."

"Sure. And keep up the monitoring." Again the little laugh.

"I will. Yes, okay," I replied, aware that I had been genuinely charmed.

"Okay. Goodbye."

Reluctantly I returned, "Goodbye," and put down the handset.

Although I was not scheduled to see her again for three months, I found myself thinking about her every day. Some mornings on my way into work I imagined I was going in to see her for a checkup. Often, relaxing with a cup of tea or sitting at the computer or standing at the water fountain, I recalled her image as she had sat and asked me questions in the examination room. And of course, the image I conjured was, at least superficially, as comprehensive as I could make it. I pictured her brown hair, from where it left her forehead to where it ended at the tip of her ponytail. I pictured her green eyes and severe expression, her nose, her smile, her chin, her ears, her neck. I pictured her hands and fingers as she had turned the pages of the folder. I pictured her legs, her skin, all of her and everything about her that I could remember, including her pink dress.

On a cold day in March I climbed the long stairs that led from the underground trolley and halted near the top to catch my breath and regain my strength. It was a little past noon. With plenty of time to make my appointment, I rested for a moment and let the remnants of winter do their work on my psyche. Then I walked half a block east, crossed the street, and approached one of the lunch carts that lined the sidewalks.

"Yes, um, I'll have the shrimp fried rice, please," I said to the woman inside. From a bright-blue cooler I pulled a bottle of spring water, placed it on the narrow counter, and stepped back to watch the woman prepare the order. She seemed to be young. A tap on my shoulder turned me around.

"Hi, Mr. Le Haley."

I took in the dark glasses and white down jacket before I said, "Oh, Dr. Feinman. Hi."

"So, what did you get?"

"Shrimp fried rice. Are you out for lunch?"

"Um-hm." Inclining her head to the side, she read the menu beside the window. When she had ordered she turned to me and said cheerily, "So, I'm seeing you at two?"

"Yes. Right."

"You're a little early."

"I guess I am," I replied. Lowering my gaze from her hair to the dark glasses, I imagined the green eyes behind them. I was staring at her and felt suddenly awkward. I asked stupidly, "Have you eaten here before?"

"No," she chuckled, "not really."

"It's pretty cold out, isn't it?" I offered.

"Oh, come on, it's gorgeous. Let's eat outside."

This plurality made my heart pound. I ventured, "Well, we could try the courtyard across the street."

"Yeah, that sounds good. I came up that way and nobody was there."

"Maybe they're not adventurous."

"Come on, it's not that cold. It's beautiful, I love it out here."

The courtyard was still empty when we arrived. Choosing a bench in the sun, we unpacked our cartons and twisted our bottle tops nearly simultaneously. The surrounding pavement radiated a pleasant heat, and as we settled in pigeons began to flutter nearby.

"So, what did you pray?" she asked as I lifted my head. "I mean, I could hardly tell, but I knew you were praying."

"I was just giving thanks for my food," I said.

"To God, huh?"

"Yes."

"To the God who gave you MS?"

"Uh-huh."

After taking a sip from her bottle of soda, she said, "You should wear sunglasses, you know. UV protection's really good, you need it, trust me. You don't have a lot of vision left."

"I know," I replied, adjusting my glasses. "I really should carry them with me."

"Yes."

Watching the plastic spoon slide from her lips, I said, "I have enough vision left to see you, though."

She chewed for a moment, swallowed, and then took another sip of soda. "It's beautiful out here."

"I know. It really is." I watched as one of the pigeons executed an elegant landing before us. His feathers seemed to be white and brown. Boldly he strode back and forth, eyeing us. I could not help marveling at him. "He's very bold," I remarked. "Do you feed the pigeons?"

"Not usually," she answered disinterestedly, removing her sunglasses and placing them between us on the bench. "Why do they always look hungry?"

"I don't know. Good question. Maybe they always are hungry. Metabolism."

"Sounds good. But maybe it's a learned technique."

"Possibly," I agreed as two others arrived. Their feathers seemed to be white and blue.

"Maybe they're playing us," she suggested, tossing the brown-and-white a hard noodle, stretching out her arm in the brilliant sunlight.

"No malice, though, right?"

"I d'know," she teased. "This guy looks kinda bad, to me."

"I think he's got a family and needs more."

Scattering the remaining noodles onto the pavement, she asked, "So, what exactly do you do at your work?"

"Editing, mostly. Well, copy-editing. I edit manuscripts and grants, stuff like that. And I do a lot of formatting."

She took another spoonful of soup, leaned back, and sighed with satisfaction. Carefully she replaced the container's lid. "I think I'm finished. That was so good. And I think I had too much."

"Soup or conversation?"

She smiled, smoothing the material of her dress. "I've enjoyed both, actually."

Watching her hands, I said, "So, your name's Roni?"

"Yes. Roni." Then she put the sunglasses on, returned the carton to its paper bag, and stood up. "So, I'll see you at two?"

"Right," I said, standing. "Sure. I'll see you then."

As she walked away I watched her until I could no longer distinguish her form, then sat again and fed the pigeons.

At just before two I checked in with the receptionist in Neurology and chose a corner seat in an alcove near the center of the spacious waiting area. Opening Word on the PDA, I accessed my journal to make an entry. I marveled that this activity had become so routine. I had begun the journal on a whim and had kept it without a significant break for nearly thirty years. At first I used little personal journals from the book store, then sketch books from the art store, then simple marble-faced composition books from the drugstore. Eventually I bought a Pocket PC PDA and continued the journal there, reveling not only in the little machine's gadgetry but in its editing capabilities. When vision loss arrived I found that backlighting and zoom made making journal entries easy. The whole method of using a PDA for journal keeping, with its wonderful portability, discreteness, and security, had become so attractive to me that I was taking the machine everywhere and making entries in the journal many times a day.

Tapping the screen with the stylus, I looked up to see a woman enter the room on one of the new electric scooters. After checking in with the receptionist, she deftly moved the scooter forward and pulled it up to a space at the end of a row of chairs. Then she just sat there quietly on her scooter, looking around occasionally, waiting to see her doctor. She was blond and wore a suit. She was thin and beautiful, and I wondered what neurological problem she might have. As I wondered the print dress of Dr. Feinman moved into my vision, and I looked up into Roni's smiling face. The smile gave me a sense of peace, and I smiled back. But then, smiles were like that, they were supposed to be like that, and everyone wanted them to be like that. They were supposed to make the recipient feel at peace. You felt good, and trusted, and were at peace, even though, of course, you knew, if you bothered to ask yourself, that a smile could mean anything, that people wore them for all kinds of reasons.

"Hi," she said at length. "Come on back."

I replaced the stylus, pushed the power button, dropped the machine into my left pant's pocket, grabbed my shoulder bag's strap, and followed her. She seemed quiet as she closed the door, and we sat down with no verbal exchange at all. When she had turned a couple of pages in the folder I said, "So, you're not wearing your lab coat."

"No, not today," she replied without looking up.

"Lab coats look professional."

"Yes, they do."

"It was fun having lunch."

It was then that she looked up at me. "Yeah," she said, nodding. "Yeah, I had a good time." Then, after glancing at another page and turning it, she sat back and looked squarely at me, as if waiting for me to say something. Then she smiled again.

"You know," I said, "by feeding that pigeon you may have just made him hungrier." This produced a brief grin so that I saw her teeth. They seemed to be small and pretty.

"You're probably right," she replied. "I guess I'll have to go back and feed him some more."

"Well, I feel responsible."

"Oh, yeah?"

"I'm the one who told you he might have a family."

"Then I guess we'll both have to go back and feed him."

I shrugged. "Okay. That would be good. Does this mean we're having a conversation?"

"You mean, are we having one now?"

"Yes, now."

"Yes," she answered. "Yes, I think it does."

She stared at me, the smile gone, and then stood up suddenly and gave the examination table's paper sheet a pat. When I was seated on the table she switched off the overhead light and came near in the semidarkness. As she slowly closed the last distance between us I sensed the vibrations from her head and from her body.

"I've often wondered," I said, "what you call that."

"An indirect ophthalmoscope," she replied, raising the instrument to look through it into my right eye. "Any change in the vision?"

Her breath was sweet, so that I wished to hear her ask the question again or say something else, anything else. I answered, "No."

Moving to my left eye, she asked, "So, you don't see this light at all?"

"No. Sorry."

"Not even a little?"

I sighed. "No."

Then she retreated a half step and said, "Well, the nerve looks really bad in that left eye, not good at all. The right's still okay. I mean, well, the nerve's very pale but not inflamed." She stepped to switch on the room's overhead and then returned. "I don't know. Actually, I don't see how you're getting around at all. It's amazing. The nerve in the right eye is really pale, and the tests show you're just not seeing much through the eye. All the quadrants are really corrupted. You've got huge blind spots all over the place. How are you even getting to work? You take the subway?"

"Yes."

"Be really careful."

"I will."

"Are the people at your work giving you a hard time or anything?"

"No, they're okay. The whole thing's made me pretty inefficient, but they seem to be patient with me. I've had a good relationship with everyone there over the years."

"That's good," she said. "Good relationship are good to have."

I nodded.

Then she sighed. "Well, let me know if you need a letter about your MS. It might help, just for them to have it on file."

"Yes. Thanks," I replied, looking as deeply as I could into the green eyes. "I'll let you know."

Chapter 2

In my office at work I launched the web browser and waited for the mail directory to appear. Then I entered my user name and password and hit Enter. Nothing new in the Inbox. Then I pressed CTRL N for another window, clicked the dropdown, clicked Google, and searched for Braille links. Knowing that another successful flare of MS could easily shut down the remaining vision had impelled me to search the internet with increasing frequency for information that might aid my navigation in the world of the blind. Adjusting the hard magnifier that hung before the screen, I scrolled through the links to Braille instruction. Since most of the sites were familiar, I searched for guide dogs and scrolled through the results for new entries. Nothing new. I pressed ALT Tab and returned to the mail directory window. At the bottom of the From column I saw the name Feinman and opened the message.

hi, it read, *it would be good to talk about your mri results. can see you soon?*

I clicked Reply and typed, *Yes. I can come down tomorrow at lunchtime, if that's okay with you. If not, maybe on Friday.*

She soon replied with, *why not do lunch first and then look at mri. can you meet me at the pigeon at noon?*

Is that a restaurant? I typed.

She replied with, *no. thats a hungry bird. see you at 12.*

At eleven forty-five the next day I stood under an umbrella, waiting for both Roni and the pigeon. It didn't seem to be a good day for a pigeon to be out. I thought of Thor and the way he had looked at me. He came to my door one evening when I lived in a row house in Olney. Absolutely ravished, he shook frantically as he devoured the two full cans of food I set before him on the patio. Then he pushed his grizzled nose against my leg, walked to a corner of the concrete, and dropped into a semicircle. It was clear that for him, whatever the past, this was to be the future. As I watched him unequivocally position himself as guardian I gave him the name Thor and admired the fierceness of his demeanor. I soon noticed, however, that he seemed to be guarding not so much the patio as my front door just above it. Apparently a mixture of pit bull and something much larger, he sported a pit bull head on a tallish muscular body. These features coupled with a speckled gray-brown coat presented a fearsome ambience. When he strode across the street to relieve himself in Fisher Park, I was certain that the wary eyes of many of my row house neighbors tracked him. Unfortunately, he was an aggressive, self-willed dog, and worse, tended to communicate more with his teeth than his voice. The little girls next door, who stood face level with his fierce teeth, daily seemed to grow more afraid of being bitten by him. I liked him and would have loved to keep him, but had concluded, after tormenting doubts, that I could neither keep him nor reasonably place him with someone else. For the sake of the little girls, for their safety and piece of mind, I decided that he could not stay. Of course, he would not simply leave. When the truck from the city shelter arrived in answer to my summons, I helped the driver corner Thor on the patio. I watched as the wire noose at the end of a long stick-like contraption was slipped around his neck and then tightened, snagging him like a criminal. I watched his pathetic struggle as he was dragged to the side of the truck, where a small metal door lay open. As he was a large dog, I helped the driver lift him to the opening of the chamber. Just before we pushed him in, the wire still tight around his neck, he turned his head to me and looked me in the face. His expression unmistakably asked, "Why have you betrayed me?" Then we thrust him in wretchedly, for he struggled to free himself from the noose. The driver slammed the door upon the dog and the stick, turned something at its end, and pulled the stick free, leaving the dog trapped in the chamber. Then the driver gave me some kind of receipt, got into the cab, and drove away. As I climbed the front steps to go into the house I saw the little girls watching me from their window, their faces filled with wonder and fear. Pushing the door open, I stood for a moment and looked down at the corner of the patio where Thor had made his home and from which he had determined to guard my life.

"Hi."

I turned to see Roni approaching under an umbrella that seemed pink or lavender. "Hi," I responded.

"Hey, what's the sad face for? You look like somebody died. Cheer up."

"Yes. Yes, I will, thanks."

"You okay?" she laughed. "I mean, that was a really sad face."

"I was . . . just remembering someone. Listen, it's kind of wet. I could get a newspaper to sit on. I haven't seen the pigeon."

"Actually, I was thinking we could go inside. The cafeteria's not bad, but there's also a food court. Okay?"

"Sure."

"*Are* you sure? Because, we could always eat in the rain."

Glad that her sarcasm was benign, I said, "No, no. It's a good idea. Sure. Let's go inside."

As we walked she leaned toward me. "Hey, cheer up."

"Sure."

"So . . . how's your color today?"

"Not bad. I'm getting most things, I think. Your umbrella's pink, right?"

"Very pink, yes."

"And your eyes are green, right?"

"Yes. Hey, that's pretty good. A lot of color-challenged people can't tell eye color very easily. That's pretty good. Was that easy for you?"

"Well, I confess I sort of wanted them to be green."

"Why?"

"I'm not sure," I replied. "I guess I thought green would be a good color for you."

"But how could you compare it to my skin? Skin's pastel. You can't distinguish pastels, I know you can't."

"Oh, I can see your skin. At least, I think I can."

17

"Well, don't be thinking too hard about that, mister."

"I'll try not to."

At the food court the lunchtime crowd kept us close. Avoiding the lines for hot dishes, we ordered sandwiches and grabbed bottles of soda, cups of ice, and bags of potato chips. After paying, we stood with our trays and looked out over the dining area. The high ceiling kept the general chatter from becoming a din, but still it seemed I needed to lean close to be heard.

"I'm afraid I can't see much here," I said. "Are there any empty tables? I'll follow you."

"I don't see one yet."

"We could always go outside."

"It's raining, stupid."

"Not too much. We could eat under umbrellas."

"Just wait."

"Or even, just one umbrella."

"Cute."

My tray seemed quite heavy. Anticipating a long wait, I looked for a place to rest it. Frustrated, I asked, "So, how do you do with parking? Do you just keep driving around the block until someone pulls out?"

"Absolutely. Car lots are expensive."

"I take the bus."

"Yeah, well, it's probably good you do. You wouldn't see the parking place, anyway. God, I hate blind people. Here, come on, here's one."

Holding my tray as level as I could, I followed her through the maze of tables. I was nervous and only hoped not to tip the contents of my tray onto some innocent person. Finally we reached a tiny table beside a low wall topped with plants. As I pulled my chair up I closed my eyes in relief that I had not spilled anything yet.

She was jubilant and wiggled happily, unfolding her paper napkin. "This is great, and it was easy."

"Easy?"

"And it's private, look at this. Come on, this is wonderful, it's a perfect table."

I acknowledged that it was. I was always happy when people helped me find things or navigate through difficult places. I told her I was grateful for her help with everything, which seemed to please her immensely. But of course, I could not tell her I was grateful for more, that I was grateful to have her sitting across from me, with pretty teeth and beautiful skin and eyes as green as ever I could want them to be.

"And no rain," she went on. "I can't believe you really wanted to go outside."

"Sorry. It was a little wet, I guess. And I guess, a little cold."

"Ye-a-h. Just a little."

"But you liked it that day we ate outside. It was cold, but you said it was gorgeous."

"But the sun was shining—all the difference in the world."

I watched her take a bite of her sandwich, then checked myself for watching too keenly.

"Are you okay?" she asked. "Can I get you anything?"

"No. I'm fine. How about you?"

She sighed. "Busy morning, totally. It's amazing what just sitting down, putting food in the mouth and swallowing does for a battered doc."

"Are you a battered doc?"

"Not really. But it has been a busy morning." Taking another bite of sandwich and pressing her back against the chair, she said, "Got a question, what do you think—" then leaning closer, "why do men look at women?"

"Maybe to see the color of their eyes better, or their skin."

She smiled. "Funny. Of course, I mean sited people."

I hesitated. I pinched a potato chip and put it in my mouth.

"As a physician I know what the science says."

"You studied," I remarked facetiously.

"I did."

I watched her lips as she chewed and then as they closed upon the straw when she took a drink. I knew I was imagining more than I was seeing. One strand of hair had freed itself from the smoothed population and hung as a spiral ornament at her right temple. I wondered if she ever wore her hair a different way. I followed the strand to its beginning, above her forehead, and then the line of her lips, in a complete circle. The table was actually too small to accommodate two people comfortably. But we were comfortable.

"That's good," I said. "A doc who didn't study might be dangerous."

"I'm not dangerous."

"Not at all?"

"No. I mean, I studied. I'm not dangerous."

"That's good. And you were saying about the science?"

"Well, the science is true, of course. That's what I was saying. It's all true, and I believe it. Not a problem."

"Okay," I said cautiously.

"This is good. I like roast beef." She was chewing again. Then she sighed and laid the sandwich down and took a chip from where I had dumped them onto my tray. "It's the usual stuff I have to eat, so I try to think it's good. It's not really bad, I just get tired of it. How's yours?"

I attempted to assemble stray pieces of turkey and bread. "Yeah, it's good, I guess."

"You don't sound convinced."

"I'm not," I replied. "So, why don't you go out for lunch every day?"

"I'm usually too busy. I'll maybe get out to a food stand once a week or so, but that's it. Lunches are mostly quick and dreary."

"So, you were saying about men looking at women."

"I suppose I should eat this sandwich, right?"

"Might make your afternoon go a little better."

She picked up the sandwich, took a bite, and then asked, "So, this kind of lighting is pretty bad for you?" She drew a little soda through her straw.

I looked around. "Um-hm."

"It's the diffused light—no hard shadows and definite lines."

"I know."

"So, you can't see my skin or the color of my eyes."

"I can see your lips on your straw. At least, I think I can."

She drew more soda into her mouth and then released the straw, not swallowing for a moment. "But you couldn't really see the pieces of your sandwich."

"No," I admitted. Then I said frivolously, "Maybe I just see what I want."

"How about getting around? Stop lights?"

"Yeah, I'm all right there. My trouble's seeing the physical stop light itself. When I locate it in my vision and fix on it I seem to see the red, yellow or green okay. I know the brain's filling in the right color for the position on the light. If they ever change the configuration of stop lights I'll be in trouble."

"Out of the color-test books you identified nothing at all."

"I know."

"But everybody's different. When vision does return, color is usually the last part to come back."

"I don't think the vision's coming back," I said.

"How do you know?"

"Just a feeling."

"You never know, everybody's different. Can you see cars when you cross the street?"

"The eye shifts around to locate them, and then it's not a problem."

"Be careful."

"I will."

"Low vision's like that. Some people say they can see a coin on the sidewalk but not the face of somebody they're talking to. Stuff like that. Can you see my face?"

"Yes," I said, "I can see your face."

"Good," she replied and then looked away.

"But then, you were pretty close during the examinations, closer than now, so maybe you're being filled in from memory. Is that okay?"

"Yes, sure," she answered, nodding vigorously. Then she asked, "What would you say vision loss means to you?"

"Well, I'm a painter, an artist, and I do photography too, and the editorial work for a regular job. Everything, really, has been vision oriented."

"So, the impact is huge."

"Um-hm."

Momentarily she asked, "What do you paint?"

I shrugged. "A little of everything. At least, I did."

"In oil?"

"Um-hm. And acrylic too, and pen-and-ink sometimes."

"And you're still working with it?"

"I get paint on my nose, but yes. Magnifiers don't really work, so I have to get close."

"What about color?"

"Yeah, color," I repeated, shaking my head. "Things end up muddy. I can still mix the colors I want. I mean, roughly. That's just knowing proportions. But as you paint, everything blends and changes, and you actually have to see the color to control it. I'm still okay with line, but color's brutal."

"Why not just go linear, skip the color, do what you can do?"

"I don't know. I think color's in my psyche. It's something I need whether I can have it or not." Our eyes seemed to meet, and I continued, "And my memory must be loaded with it, so I just try to fake it, take a guess at it and then let it go."

"You don't seem like a faker. Maybe a different word would be better. Maybe you're just too persistent."

"Maybe."

"Well, you still do it. That's great. Are you in a gallery?"

"Yes. But they don't know about my vision. They're mostly carrying my older things right now. I also show at a small art club in the city. They're, like, a historic art club."

"As long as you can still do it, just keep at it. I'd like to see your things sometime."

After a moment I said, "Do you do anything in the arts?"

"I've tried some drawing with charcoal. Nothing great. I took it in college. Sometimes I draw for relaxation."

"And that works. I mean, it relaxes you?"

She chuckled. "Actually, no. I guess it's more like a distraction for me from all the medical journals I have to read, maybe."

"I can see that. And charcoal's neat. I like charcoal."

She wrinkled her nose. "Messy."

I nodded. "Yep, it is. And don't breathe it—not good. I've breathed too much of it, I think."

"I can imagine. Has anybody said you wheeze at night, in your sleep?"

I tried searching her eyes at this, but gave it up and replied simply, "Only my dogs would know."

"Oh."

"So, can I see what you've done?"

She gave her cup a shake, and it seemed that we both listened to the rattle of the ice. Then she put the cup down. "You want to? Sure. They're nothing great."

"You said that, yes. I'd love to see your things."

Her forefinger went up. "Okay, but you can't be critical, no harsh stuff."

"You're sensitive."

"Yes."

"No, I'll just look. I won't say a thing, if you want."

She shrugged in reply.

"So, why *do* men look at women? Or women look at men?"

She smiled. "Maybe I'll withdraw the question."

Wishing I could see more of her face, I asked, "Do you think mystical reality emasculates science?"

"Not possible."

"No?"

"How could it emasculate science when it is subject to the scrutiny of science?"

"Maybe," I posed, "the mystical world is autonomous."

"You don't think much of science, do you?"

"Sure I do. It's wonderful. It's certainly helping me. But in the face of mystical reality it seems a little lame."

She was incredulous. "Lame?"

"Science can't control the mystical realm, even in the slightest."

"So?"

"Science has never captured or conquered the mystical realm."

"So?"

"Scientists in general seem to think the reality of anything and everything is subject to their process of observation, theory, testing, understanding, and whatever. But in spite of all kinds of pronouncements science has made against mystical reality, the mystical realm still continues to operate totally unhindered. Science has no power whatever over the mystical realm."

"So?"

"Well, so, that's lame."

"Science saves lives and makes lives better. That's not lame."

"No, no, not in relation to disease. No. There it's very powerful. Look how it's helped me. Sure. And it even helps me to paint. I mean, the paints were developed through technology."

"But?"

"Well, I think science should resolve to coexist in peace with the mystical realm. In other words, scientists should quell their own ego and admit that science represents only one facet of human understanding. Science should simply get rid of its idea that the existence and nature of reality are subject to its goofy methodological process."

"Goofy? As in discovering penicillin?"

"No. As in determining mystical reality. That's where it's goofy."

"But that process *is* science."

"So, change the definition."

After a moment she said, "Science is my world."

"But it's not comprehensive or you wouldn't have posed the question in the first place. Look, I'm not against science, I'm really not."

"But?"

"But it's not fun."

She stared at me. "Oh please. Boy, you throw curve balls. *Fun?*"

My sandwich was now a heap of unidentifiable parts on my plate. Clumsily I pushed its remnants together and then looked back up at Roni. Her face had withdrawn into the shadows of my blindness, and for some reason, at least momentarily, memory was failing to fill it back in.

"Well," I said, "magic is fun. To me, science is, like, business or facts. Magic is fun."

"Do you mean occult?"

"No, no. I mean magic in the sense of the mysteries of life without thinking about them. You know—life and love and beauty."

"But science *is* fun, for scientists."

"I suppose," I admitted. "But it has its limits."

"Meaning?"

"Meaning that sometimes people who know science, like yourself, find themselves curious about things other than hormones."

Crossing her arms and leaning both elbows on the table, she said, "Okay, I'll play." And then, quite beautifully, "Why do you think men look at women?"

"I think because they're beautiful."

She smiled inquisitively. "Which?"

"The women."

"Oh."

Oddly, her eyes no longer seemed to be green, but simply a strange gray, and her skin tones were gone, and she looked like everything else in the room—blurry, broken up. I wanted to keep her the way I had seen her, but was powerless to do so.

"Listen," I said at length, "don't we have an appointment? The MRI results? Don't you have to get back?"

She glanced at her watch. "Uh, yes, right, I do. The MRI showed the brain lesions are a little worse but still typical for functioning patients with MS."

"Will the lesions damage the brain?"

Momentarily she replied, "No, no, your brain's okay. a little screwball, maybe, but okay. Don't worry about the lesions. You have spinal lesions, too, but don't worry about it. Everything's typical. Just keep taking the meds. Hopefully they'll do what they're supposed to and you won't lose the rest of your vision."

"Yes. I hope they do." I raised my shoulders and let them drop. "Who knows?"

Then she smiled and said, "Your eyes are hazel."

Chapter 3

A few days later I climbed the dark stairway at the Walnut-Locust stop of the Broad Street subway and walked south to Spruce and then west. There was something delicious about the brilliantly sunlit atmosphere, that made me stop occasionally to sample it. Someone must have been having a wedding, for I saw ribbons, flowers, and some kind of balloon-marked sign beside a limousine parked along the street.

Roni's email invitation to come and see her apartment and drawings had said I could arrive anytime during the day. She must have been concerned for my safety, for the message had urged me, in all caps, to take my time and not hurry. And I had been faithful in doing just that, even deliberately slowing my pace to appreciate the weather. But then, out of sheer habit, I pressed the button on my talking watch and suddenly found myself hurrying toward a little bakery I knew of near Rittenhouse Square. There I bought some sort of cake and two large raisin cookies. Once outside I began to hurry even more, going nowhere and yet somewhere I wanted to go to very much.

At the street number Roni had given I stepped onto a whitish slab, turned a shiny handle, and entered a foyer at the bottom of a dark stairway. With the door still open I leaned close to the mailboxes and pressed the button under Feinman. Then pulling the door securely closed I waited for a response. At the sound of a door opening I looked up into the darkness and listened as someone descended. Then Roni came into view.

"Hi, Stanly," she said. "Come on up."

It was the first time she had called me by my first name, and she might as well have kissed me. "Hey, Roni," I said. Then she turned and I followed, but soon had to stop. "I'm sorry, but I just can't see anything here."

"It's okay. Here, take my hand."

I shifted the package and reached out. It was the first time I had touched her. At the landing we passed through the still-open door of the apartment. Our hands came apart and she closed the door. The room was well lit, and I felt myself relax. "Hey, it's a little brighter in here. This is great."

"Yeah. The stairs are dark. We need another light out there. There's one at the bottom, but it doesn't do much good during the day. Don't worry, I'll walk you down. What's this?"

I handed her the bag. "Yeah, it's from a bakery just off Rittenhouse Square."

"Thank you. Wonderful. Hey, want some coffee? I'll put a pot on, okay? Or maybe tea."

I had been looking at her hair, so replied, "That'd be good, sure."

"Which?"

"Coffee, yes."

On a leather couch that rested perpendicular to a tall, curtainless window we sat with coffee and the cookies and slices of the cake. I knew as I looked at her that the image of her sitting there would never leave me. The white sneakers, the faded jeans, the reddish shirt, the loosened hair, the face. And then the voice, enhancing the image. All of it went into my mind and indeed never left.

As she brought a knee up and turned a little more toward me I remarked, "That's a bright window."

"I know," she replied, glancing at it. "I was surprised, actually. When I took the apartment it was overcast, almost dark out, but the day I moved in, there it was, the Mediterranean sun. It doesn't last long, though. And I'm usually at the hospital, anyway."

"You like the sun."

"Yeah. I do. How about you?"

"I'm kind of a rain person. It looks like a great apartment."

"Thanks. There's even an alley and a place to park."

"You have a car?"

"Yep. A little one. I didn't grow up in the city and I like to get away sometimes."

"Where're you from?"

"Doylestown."

"Oh, close by. Wow, that's gorgeous up there. Do you ever go to the folk festival at the museum grounds?"

Shifting a little she said, "I try to go every few years. Just for nostalgia, I think. Yeah, it's really, as *you* say, fun. Actually it's next Saturday, I think."

"Really? I didn't know. I went a few years ago and it was wonderful. I loved it and didn't get to see enough."

"It's always on Mother's Day weekend. Even if it rains. Yeah, it makes a great day to get away. So, do you want to go?"

"Uh, well, yeah. Sure. That'd be great, yeah. How're you going up?"

She shook her head. "Oh, drive. I mean, we could take the train, if you want. But I love to drive—open road, and everything."

"Sure."

"That way we can bring stuff back if we buy anything. It'll be good. We'll make a day of it."

"Sure, okay." Then, pointing to a picture on the wall, I said, "I saw your drawing there. I liked it."

"Thanks. Yeah, drawing's a meditative activity for me, when it goes right."

"I know."

"Therapeutic."

I chuckled. "I know." I looked at her shirt and followed it down to her jeans. "Any favorite artists?"

"Oh, I don't know. I guess I like Klimt a lot. And maybe O'Keefe."

"Yes, Klimt's really interesting. I saw a great photo of him online. Dora Kallmus, I think."

"I've seen it. What's the name again?"

"Dora Kallmus. Maybe I've got it wrong." Fascinated with the loosened hair, I followed it from her shoulders to her forehead. "Have you done any painting?"

She shook her head. "I wish."

"Just journals, huh?"

"Neurology, neurology. Enough."

"What else do you wish?"

"What?"

"You said *I wish.* What else do you wish."

"Well, it wasn't really a wish. But, not much, I think. I don't believe wishes mean much, anyway."

Looking toward the picture on the wall, I asked, "Was that done in a class?"

"Uh-huh. He was a good model, or at least seemed to be, I don't know. He never moved. He was very good." Her eyes went to the picture as she took a bite of cookie and then a sip of coffee.

"So, it was undergrad?"

"Yep. A lot of interesting people."

"Did art help you with anatomy in med school?"

"No, I don't think so. I don't see how it could've. Med school's pretty thorough."

"But you liked it, right? I mean, art?"

She grinned. "Yes, I do, a lot. Do you do figures?"

"I have. Mostly landscapes and abstracts now. I've sold a lot of nudes over the years, though."

"You have a model?"

"No, I work from photographs." Then I added, "I mean, I take pictures of a model first, yeah."

"A professional model?"

"Not really. Well, you know, just women I've thought would be beautiful to paint."

"How does that work?"

"Uh, well, they pose, I take some photos and then do a series of paintings."

"Will many women do that?"

At length I replied, "I haven't really asked many. Just a few, actually. You know, over the years."

Then she asked, "Is there someone now?"

I shook my head. "No. I mean, I still have the photographs. But, no. There's no one now. I haven't done a new set of nude photos for a number of years, since before I lost my vision. And I haven't actually completed one of the paintings in probably six or seven years."

"Do you have any I could see?"

"Finished paintings?"

"Um-hm."

"Sure." And then she seemed to shift to another thought, so I said, "You know, historically representation of the nude in art has been criticized a lot. Some have charged that it smacks of the classics and isn't really modern, that it's a cheap trick and exploitation."

"What do you think?"

"I think the creativity of a critical mind is just about boundless."

"But aren't you just criticizing the critics?"

"Yeah, but it isn't my job to sit around making things up about them. But I guess it doesn't really matter. Artists pretty much just do what they want, anyway. They always have. Especially if you tell them they can't do it."

"Is that good?"

"You tell me."

She made a face. "This coffee's cold. Here, give me your cup. Want some hot?"

I handed her the cup as she passed. "Maybe half a cup."

And then she disappeared, and it was as if she had never existed. I heard the rustling of her movements in the kitchen and the clinking of the cups as she rinsed and then filled them, but it was as if she had gone forever from my life. I had caused her to leave, and like Thor, she would never come back.

When she returned with the coffee and had sat down again, she said, "Are you okay?"

"Yes. Sure."

"You look a little funny."

"I'm fine. Thanks."

Then I took a small piece of the cake and held it on a paper napkin in my hand. And as she did the same her movements told me she had come back. She was blurry, but I could see her. She was there, sitting not far away, breathing, smiling, eating the cake. But then, she had not been truly gone. If only someone who was truly gone could come back like that. How wonderful that would be.

"Are you sure you're okay?" she asked.

"Yes. This is good. Thanks." Then I thought that I had perhaps stayed too long. But I had not seen the drawings, which was why I had been invited in the first place. I said, "So, can I see your drawings?"

"Oh, sure." From behind a door to what seemed to be her bedroom (although I could still see her) she retrieved a black portfolio and opened it across a corner of the coffee table. "Now, you can't be mean," she laughed. "I was just having fun."

"Hey, that's when an artist really tells the truth."

"You think?"

As I turned the pages I noted the scent of hairspray. "Aqua Net?"

"Yeah," she chuckled.

"It's a great fixative." I turned the sheets slowly, then sat back, leaving the last drawing face up. "Hey, I like them. Really neat. Who's the woman?"

"Actually, the teacher. The model didn't show up for the final class, so she just said 'oh, what the hell,' pulled her shirt off, and sat for us."

I shook my head. "Wow. That's quite a teacher."

"She was, yeah."

"But it looks like the class wasn't the first time you'd worked in art."

"No. No, I'd drawn before."

I took a sip of coffee and pushed my back into the cushion. "So, what took you to med school? I mean, it seems like you could have been anything you wanted. Why a neurologist?"

"Good question, really. I think I was always kind of meant to be a doctor, or maybe just wanted to be. I don't know. That's all I can say. I've worked hard at it, though. I'd like to be really good." As she spoke I thought of Thor and how he had been captured, thrust into the chamber and taken away. I saw him in his aloneness scrunched up there in the darkness. I saw his eyes and in them the deepest sense of the loss of everything. Then I heard her saying, "I always gravitated toward medicine, I think. Was it that way with you and art?"

"I suppose," I said. "I don't know. But, why neurology?"

"The field somehow interested me when I was in medical school. I'm not sure what the attraction was. Maybe I thought I'd be safe. You know, not have to get so close to the patients."

"Safe."

She shook her head. "I don't know. Maybe I thought it would be less messy."

"Is it?"

"I don't know," she said again. "I didn't just want the easy way. I've worked really hard."

"It's not easy?"

"No, it isn't. Even as a resident you have to look into the face of someone with an aggressive brain tumor, knowing they're going to die."

"You could always quit. Take another art class."

"Yeah."

"Go to Italy, sit in the sun, draw the Mediterranean shore."

She gave a half laugh. "Yeah, I suppose I could."

"Do you ever see children?"

"No. I couldn't do pediatrics. I could never do that. We see teens and up, and that's hard enough. It's, like, you're the one who's supposed to help them and you have to give them the odds against their survival."

"But you're okay with it?"

"So far," she said. "You either become a little callous—I mean, you *do*—you just have to. Or you get sensitized. For some docs, having a patient die is a weight they can't get rid of. They carry it and carry it. And then it happens again, and it's too much. But you kind of know if you'll be able to handle it, just by being in medicine and working through the process of becoming a doc. So, by the time you go into practice, you *know*."

"Yeah. But nothing's as simple as that."

"Well, sometimes things develop and docs can't handle it. It's rare, but it happens."

"What do they do?"

She hesitated. "Retire early. Do something else. Or get away from the patients. Become an advisor or something."

"But you'll be okay?"

"I think so."

"Go the distance?"

"I think so," she said, as if to herself.

Chapter 4

The next Saturday, under a partially clouded sky, we drove north on 309 to Montgomeryville and then veered off toward Doylestown. The back seat carried nothing but a sweater and two umbrellas.

I looked over as she cracked her window for fresh air. I had been trying to follow her lips whenever she spoke, or watch the movements of her hands.

"Highway driving always makes me sleepy," she said. "I don't know how truckers do it."

"Want to stop for some coffee or something?"

"No, I'll be fine. It's not that far."

"You know, if we get separated I think I could actually find you, with the stripes on that shirt."

"Top," she corrected.

"Right."

"Too bold?"

"The stripes? No. No, you look really nice."

"Thanks. So do you."

"Uh-oh. I'm not sure that compliment was genuine, doc."

"As genuine as yours."

"I don't think so," I replied, looking at the highway.

"Do you get up here much?"

"Not really," I said. "I used to drive up about, oh, maybe once a year. I guess I could come up on the R5. I should really do that. Come up just for the day. I don't know."

"So, are your dogs going to be okay for the whole day?"

"Oh, sure. They'll be all right. They're great dogs."

"What do you think they're doing now?"

"Right now? Who knows? Probably sleeping."

Switching lanes, she accelerated until we had overtaken a lumbering minivan. "They're inside?"

"I would have left them out, but it looked like it might rain."

"They don't like the rain?"

"No. I don't know why, but they don't." For just an instant, I saw Thor as he struggled in the catcher's wire. I saw him run into the corner of the patio and, desperate to escape the tightened noose, push his head into the stone front of the house. "I'm glad I left them in. It might rain."

She glanced at me and then looked back through the windshield. "Think we'll need our umbrellas?"

"No. I don't think so."

"If you leave them out, do you chain them?"

I looked over at her and then back at the highway. "No. No, I never chain them."

"Some people are really against it."

"Yes."

"But don't they ever, like, wet the rug?"

"They're really good about it." I said. "They wait every day until I get home from work, and when they can't they go in the basement. I think they'll be okay today, though. They all went before I left."

"I've never been to East Oak Lane. What's it like?"

"Lots of trees. Beautiful old houses."

"You live in a single?"

"Yes, ma'am. Are you jealous?" I teased.

She tugged at her cap. "Yep. Just a little."

"I used to live in a row. In Olney. No yard at all."

"You had dogs?"

"No. Not then. A visitor once. Well, sort of a visitor. He wasn't there long." And when I felt her looking at me I added, "It didn't work out."

After a moment she said, "I'm sure they'll be fine."

In Doylestown we were fortunate to find street parking directly across from the museum. Roni slipped the car expertly into the space, shut the engine down, and closed her eyes. I was incredulous when she said, "I hate parking. Stomach ache, every time."

Shaking my head, I said, "Why? That was perfect."

She did not reply, but pulled the rearview mirror and looked at her face, not in the usual way, but as if to ask who she was. Then she pushed the mirror back and we left the sweater and the umbrellas, crossed the street, and climbed the gentle slope to the entrance gate. Once inside, we stood in the shade of a huge tree to scan our exhibit guides.

"Too small," I said and dropped the guide into a trash basket. "What's it say?"

"Aw. Guess you need me."

"Guess I do. You'd think a sans serif bold font would be more appropriate."

"Poor blind man, lost 'is sight in the service of King George."

As her eyes ran down the list of exhibits and events I tried in vain to discern their particular shade of green, eventually contenting myself with following the lines of the ball cap until its strap connected under the ponytail. "So, what shall we see?"

Slipping the guide into her cross-slung purse, she said, "Well, there's too much here, actually. So, why don't we just walk and see what we find?"

"Sounds good."

She closed her eyes and took a deep breath. "Every time I come here, I just love it."

I continued in the teasing mood, "So, you don't just think about medicine?"

"No. Sometimes I think about fun."

"Wow. I'm impressed."

Then she took my arm in hers. "Come on," she said. And as we turned and began to walk she leaned into me and said, "It's a beautiful morning."

I looked up at the trees and the sky. "Yes, it is," I returned. "By the way, let me know if you see anything I might trip over."

"Will do."

The quaint rolling grounds of the museum had been meticulously transformed into a maze of tantalizing exhibits. Tables, booths, performing stages, and reenactment areas converted what normally would have made for an easy stroll around the museum into what now made for an arduous hike. The pervading atmosphere of colonial and early-American life, created through costumed cooks, artisans, and performers, seemed nearly to engulf our senses.

After an hour of circular wandering I slumped wearily onto the first empty bench we found, while Roni placed an order for funnel cake and coffee. I could not believe how tired I was. It was unusual for me to ignore the warnings of approaching fatigue, but walking beside her, talking with her, engaging the very aura of her person, had so distracted me that now it was as if every cell in the battery had gone dead at once. When she came to sit beside me I watched helplessly as she unwrapped the funnel cake and removed the tops from the coffee. The simple sounds of paper and plastic seemed distant, enigmatic.

"Here," she said.

I took the cup and put it under my nose. "Oh. Unbelievable."

"And here." Carefully she pulled away a piece of the powdered cake and handed it to me. When she saw that I waited for her, she said sharply, "Oh, come on. You're not that old."

"I was just being courteous."

"I know. Just eat."

I watched as she took a bite of the cake and chewed it. "Aren't your feet going to get tired in sandals?"

She took another bite of the cake, chewed for a moment, and said, "I think you're the one who had to rest."

"Uh-huh. You're right." Watching her mouth as she ate, I said, "The lady is right."

Then she asked, "So, would you like to make gender a nonissue?"

"No. I don't think I would," I answered. "Would you?"

She sipped the coffee. "No. Okay, let's keep it."

"You can still be a lady?"

"Well, maybe just a girl."

"So, what does the doctor order for the rest of the morning?"

"Listen," she said gently, "if you don't stop looking at me I'm going to spill my coffee."

"Oh, my. Staring?"

"Uh-huh. You do that, you know."

"Yes. Sorry," I said and took another bite of the cake.

"You look at just about every beautiful woman that crosses your road. They're always beautiful. And you look at me all the time. You never stop."

"Oh. Yeah. Well. You're right, I do."

At length she asked, "So, how much can you see today?"

"I can see enough, don't worry."

"Well," she said, "I have noticed that you also look at men and children and dogs just about the same way."

"And how is that?"

"Maybe aesthetically. Who knows?"

"Oh, so I can get away with it since I'm an artist?"

"Well," she said slyly, "maybe just a little."

"So, I look at you the same way, huh?"

She was pleased. "Just about. Maybe there's more."

"Shall we keep gender, then?"

"Prob'ly would be good," she said, her eyes following the crowd.

"Sounds good, doctor." I wiped my hands on a napkin and took a drink of the half-cooled coffee.

She broke off a piece of the funnel cake and rubbed her fingers and thumb together. "But if we keep gender, maybe we could make profession a nonissue."

"Well, if you're not a doctor you can't consider my health."

"That's right. And if you're not an artist you can't consider the way I look."

"Like I was blind?"

"Yep," she teased. "Just like you were blind."

"I don't know if I could live with that."

"With what? Blindness?"

"No," I said. "I didn't mean blindness."

She smiled tenderly, so very tenderly, and touched my arm. "Come on. Let's walk."

In the early afternoon, plumped from a lunch of spit-roasted beef and at least two varieties of pie, we sat at the end of a long folding table under a canvas awning and waved away curious flies. To a tapping drum and tooting fife a group of militia, muskets shouldered, marched past us and disappeared into the crowds. On a paved rise a hay wagon, returning from a round-the-grounds tour, stopped to allow its riders to jump down. Men, women and children in various American costumes sauntered to and from the lunch area.

When a two-o'clock sun painted color between the streaks of clouds, we wandered into an exhibit of colonial hearth cooking and took seats on a split-log bench. Somewhat reluctantly, we accepted samples of nut bread from a large bowl held out by a large woman in a large apron.

"This crust looks so good," Roni said to me in a low voice, breaking off a small piece and putting it into her mouth. And then, as the woman moved to the people on the benches behind us, "but I don't think I can eat any more today. I simply never eat this much. And it all seems to be cake and pie and bread. I mean, enough already."

"I know," I agreed. "But it's been a lot of fun, hasn't it?"

"Yes. Fun. But maybe we could get back to science. And science says calories. And I don't need the fat."

I didn't look at her. "You're not fat. You're not even close."

"Well, I certainly don't want to get there."

"Do you bake bread?" I asked.

"Not really. I *have*. But it wasn't great. I think I'll get a bread maker. Do you bake?"

"I'm not a bread person," I said. "I like cookies. To go with tea. I *am* a tea person."

"What about all the coffee we seem to end up with?"

"I know."

"What kind of tea?"

"Oolong, mostly."

"Oh. Black Dragon."

"You know that? Do you know any other Chinese?"

"Nope. That's it. I'm a coffee drinker. I like coffee."

When the woman offered us another bowl for sampling, we declined and again took to the narrow grassy lanes that crisscrossed the festival. The combination of sun and clouds presented a glorious canopy to walk under. In any one area the ground was fairly level, and it was only occasionally that her hand came out to guide me around an obstacle. For a time we didn't say anything, but contented ourselves with listening to the simple sounds we made as we moved through the crowd or examined an exhibit's artifacts.

But then I said, "You've been looking at me."

"I'm trying to picture you without a beard," she replied.

"Well, that should be easy. It's a short beard."

"I don't know. Even short beards can be deceptive."

"Maybe it's not a beard. Maybe it's a tactile tattoo."

"Very good. Little long for that, I think."

"I've been doing some wondering about you myself. Just for fun."

With her eyes half closed, she said, "Maybe you have too much fun sometimes."

"It's possible," I admitted. "Do you like to cook?"

"Wow. That's abrupt. Sometimes. Not too fancy. Do you?"

"Spaghetti. Simple stuff. Leaves more time for the studio."

She looked away briefly and then said, "I cook for myself. It's a break from restaurants."

"Breaks are good."

"Do you see your painting as a break?"

"No. More like, a long-term thing. I'm not sure how I see my regular job. It pays the bills. I think movies are my break. I love movies."

"You go to theaters?"

"Not much, anymore. They look mostly black and white now. It's the reflected light. But on a high-definition TV screen I can see everything. Well, just about."

"Sure. I've heard that," she said. "Backlighting seems to help."

"Is that a professional observation?"

Her nose twitched and she gave me a curious look. "Oh, no. Not at all."

"Good thing, doctor."

"Movies *are* a good break, though. I like movies. But they steal time."

"Right."

"What about the domesticity thing?"

"I don't know. Part fantasy, part reality. I'm not sure."

She was quiet. "Everything's a fantasy."

"Wow. Sounds almost mystical."

"Oh, I can be mystical, don't worry."

"So much for science," I said.

"No, no. Science is good. I actually *want* to be a neurologist."

"Well, you're there, sweetheart. You're certainly there. Behold the neurologist."

Again the curious look. Then she asked, "What did you call me?"

"A neurologist."

"No."

"Sweetheart?" And when she nodded and lifted her chin, I asked, "Is that a term I shouldn't use?"

Drawing a finger across her eyebrow, she replied, "It doesn't matter."

Then again we fell silent and simply wandered. There were so many fantasies to entertain us. Spindle-chair making, cabin building, wool weaving, blacksmithing. When she took a seat at a presentation of quilting techniques I moved on alone to a roped area where Border Collies were being shown. As I approached a woman in a cowboy hat was calling commands to a black-and-white. At the sharp report of muskets fired in unison by the nearby militia, the collie, awaiting with fixed eyes the trainer's next command, did not move. The audience gathered around the rope had been startled, but not the dog. Then I heard Roni's voice at my side.

"Hey," she said, "what is it with boys and dogs?"

For a moment I was unable to answer. Then I said, "Hi."

"Yep. Boys and dogs."

"We've kept gender and tossed profession. Maybe we'd better deal with age."

"Wouldn't you like to be a little boy again and have a dog and a fishing pole?"

I looked at the collie and then laughed. "In some ways, maybe. That doesn't sound bad, at all."

"Not in every way?"

"No. Too much nonsense. I didn't expect you so soon. You looked really interested in the quilting stuff."

"Yeah, I don't know," she said aimlessly.

"What? Domesticity overload?"

"More like, fantasy, I think."

"But you said everything was a fantasy."

"Yeah. Yeah, I think it is." Then she sighed and took my arm in hers.

"Hey," I ventured, "I think you're about five eight. Tell me if I'm wrong."

"Oh, great. Now we have to make height a nonissue."

"So, how tall do you think I am?"

"Five nine," she replied slyly. "I know all about you. I have your chart, remember."

"Ah, by that you just made profession an issue again."

"Well, I can't not remember your height."

"But you said my chart. That's profession."

"So, you're going to start looking at me from an artist's perspective again, huh?"

"A-ah, that would be nice," I said, giving her arm a squeeze of my own. "That would be very nice."

Chapter 5

On the following Saturday I awoke with a headache and pulled the pillow over my head, shutting out light and sound. I thought of how it must be both horrible and wonderful for the deaf-blind to awake in the morning. To hear nothing. To see nothing. To be totally vulnerable, and yet totally secure. These headaches and the other flu-like symptoms that often accompanied them were not unusual following an interferon injection the night before. The regular remedy of two extra-strength pain relievers on an empty stomach brought the expected respite, and within half an hour I was sitting up in bed with most of the morning before me.

Following a good face washing and teeth brushing I pulled on my painting clothes and sat on the bed to tie my shoes. Through this routine Helga lay stretched across her mat in the corner, with half-closed eyes and an expression that said she knew the cues. Her sad eyes followed the movements as I fastened my belt, clipped my keys to a loop, and dropped my penknife into the right front pocket. When I retrieved the Tokarev from beside the pillow and brought its hammer from half-cock to full-rest, she opened her eyes wide, sat up, and then followed me to the studio. Sono emerging from the middle room and Ragnar from the bathroom joined us on the landing.

In the studio I unlocked the steel cabinet and exchanged the old piece for a snub-nosed three fifty-seven, which I holstered inside my waistband, just a little farther than midway back on the right. I made a belt adjustment to accommodate the fat cylinder and relocked the cabinet. Then the four of us descended the back stairs to the kitchen.

By this time all three dogs were frantic to get out into the yard. Crowding onto the basement landing, they pressed against me as I turned the deadbolt and threw the two mechanical bolts. Grudgingly they squeezed around the inner door as I opened it inward, and then at the first crack of the outer door they blasted through. Why it had to be this way I did not know. But it always seemed to work.

It was not until eleven o'clock that I dropped the number fourteen brush into its murky water and took the palette to the basement to spray it off in the stationary tub. As always, the descent wasn't so bad but the return climb to the second floor was brutal and made me more determined to install a utility sink in the studio. Resting at the first landing, I let the dogs in and went into the kitchen to get them a biscuit. I considered it lucky that the doorbell sounded then, before I had climbed to the studio. Instantly the dogs launched an attack on the inner front door. Through the panes I could see Roni standing outside. Closing this door behind me to shut the dogs in, I crossed the enclosed porch, threw the security bolts, and opened the Plexiglas-protected outer front door.

"Hey, Roni. A surprise." I said as she gave a little wave. "Come in."

"I will, thanks."

When I had returned the bolts home I said, "It's neat you've come. You can meet the dogs and see my studio."

"Yeah," she said, nodding. "That's a good idea." Then, satisfied that her note of sarcasm had not escaped me, she added, "I guess I just wanted to crash in."

"See what I was really like, huh?"

"Maybe a little." She eyed the dogs. "For their heads to reach that glass they must be big."

"Oh, not too big, really."

"Is that Helga? That's a massive head. Look at those ears."

"Okay, just stand here and I'll bring them out. Don't touch them, okay? Just let them sniff."

"Fine."

"You won't try to touch them, right?"

She shook her head. "No, Stanly, I won't. No."

"Okay."

"Don't worry," she added. "I actually like dogs."

Half an hour later we sat on plastic lawn chairs on the back patio and absorbed the rays of the May sun. With Raggie and Sono playing a rather serious game of tag and Helga sleeping between our chairs, we sipped iced grape juice and occasionally waved at a fly.

When Helga lifted herself and walked away Roni asked, "How much do they weigh?"

"Well, Helga's been over a hundred, but her hips aren't great so the vet told me to reduce her food. She's down to about eighty-seven right now. Ideal is about eighty-two."

"She's absolutely huge."

"That's mainly because she's so long."

"She's a full German Shepherd?"

"Uh-huh."

Her eyes followed the long, silvered tail as Helga disappeared around the corner of the house. "And, is it *Ragnar* and *Sono*? What kind are they?"

"Raggie's a Shepherd-Lab and Sono's an Akita. They're about sixty apiece."

"Raggie's all black?"

"Except for a few bird dog-type markings."

"Her head's just like a German Shepherd's."

"I know."

"And Sono looks more like a wolf than a wolf does. Have you ever been bitten?"

"No, not really. A few slashes, but nothing serious. I've heard that dog bites can be pretty bad, though."

She grimaced. "I know. I haven't been bitten, but I've seen a few ER cases. My dad liked dogs. He was always saying a good dog was like a loaded gun."

"I've heard that," I said, nodding. "It seems like a good analogy. But some people would've said a *bad* dog was like a loaded gun."

"But my dad liked dogs."

"Did you like your dad?" I asked.

"Yes, I did. He was a great guy. I think, to him, no dogs were bad. Do you think there are bad dogs?"

"Only from a human perspective. I think the problem is the interface connecting canine and human behavior. And the problem is generated by the misunderstanding on both sides. The dog doesn't understand the human, and the human doesn't understand the dog. The dog bites the human, and the human says the dog is bad."

"So, no bad dogs?"

"I don't think so."

"Don't tell me—bad people, though, right?"

"Yes."

Wiping condensation from her glass, she said, "But people can also be good, right?"

"Yes, they can."

"I'm glad to hear you say that." Reaching to pat my arm she said, "You have nice dogs." Then she looked up through the tree limbs. "Umm. It's nice here. It's beautiful. So, before I crashed in, what were your plans today?"

"I was going to work in the studio."

"Paint?"

"Uh-huh."

"So, I interrupted you?"

I shook my head. "Not really. I'm glad you came."

"Sure?"

"I'm very sure."

After a moment she said, "I have to do some shopping this afternoon. Want to come?"

"Yes."

"But I'd like to see your paintings." When I didn't reply she asked, "Is it okay? Do you show them?"

"Sure. I don't mind."

"Okay. Then you can help me get some things at the market."

"That would be fun."

"Why not get lunch there, do the shopping, and maybe go to a movie or something?"

I nodded. "That would be even more fun." I imagined following her around a store, pushing the cart, watching her movements. But now she seemed to be looking from my T-shirt to my pants, both of which were covered with dried paint.

"Do you ever wear anything but jeans?" she asked.

"Sometimes."

"I mean, I've never seen you wear anything else."

"They're comfortable and the only thing that seems to fit right. I can wear something else, if you want."

"Were you a hippie?"

"No, I wasn't. I'm just kind of stuck on comfort. I don't see much point in dressing up. I mean, what *is* the point?"

"It might show," she said noncommittally, "that you're taking things seriously."

I put my hands together, interlocking the fingers. "Yeah, it might *show* it."

"Not important?"

"Not a lot."

"So, I imagine you're not a Valentine's Day kind of guy, huh?"

"Not really."

"What about at work? You never dress up for work?"

"No."

"Don't they say anything?"

"No. They overlook it, I think."

"And church? I know you go to church, you say grace. Do you wear jeans to church?"

"Uh-huh."

Then she asked, "Could I see your wardrobe? I mean, would you mind?"

"Sure. Can I see yours?"

Staring at me, she replied, "Sure. Why not." Then she gave a sigh of exasperation and looked up through the tree limbs again.

As if to complete the scene, Helga returned to the patio, circled our chairs once, and without acknowledging us lay at our feet. With her head between her paws, she gave a long, pathetic sigh, her eyes tracking Raggie and Sono as they sniffed for squirrels at the corner of the garage. She did not stir when I nudged her side with my shoe.

Roni looked down at her. "She seems so sad."

"That she is. She always has been. She's very protective. She nearly killed Raggie and Sono when I brought them home for the first time. Now she just tolerates them."

"How did you get her?"

"She had been returned to her breeder for supposedly killing two of her new owner's prize exotic roosters and then nipping at a boy. The breeder was going to put her down, as they say, and offered her to me. So, I adopted her and brought her home. It was funny. When I got her here she just went around prowling the place. She sniffed the whole house and yard, just once, and then kind of settled in, like she knew this would now be her home."

"What about killing the roosters?"

"She may have. Actually, I didn't care. But she didn't seem like that kind of dog. Raggie's caught two squirrels, and she killed both of them. But when Helga caught one, or cornered it over there by the door, she held it down with her paw and then just let it go. I saw her. It was amazing. She chased it into the corner and then just held it down."

"But she bit a boy?"

"Well, she is protective. And I don't want her to hurt anybody. So, I've got to be kind of careful."

"I would think so," she said, fixing her eyes on Helga's sleeping head. "But she could have behavioral problems."

"So could I. And you're sitting here drinking grape juice with me."

She made a click with her tongue. "Not quite the same. People are a little more readable, I think."

I didn't reply. Then I said, "Once, maybe about a month after she came, I took her out to the front yard on a Saturday morning. I just, you know, wanted to work on my PDA and have her out there with me. Anyway, I put the lawn chair just before the grass sloped to the sidewalk. For awhile she was quiet, and I thought she was asleep. So, I just sat there, working away. But then my neighbors came around the corner. They were just taking a walk. I didn't see them. Then, right out of nothing, Helga just blew up and ferociously charged them. I mean, the noise was incredible. She didn't bite them or anything. She never touched them. But she came so close. Apparently she had waited until they reached a certain point on the sidewalk and then charged them. Well, wisely, they froze and waited for me to come and get her. I apologized over and over. I mean, I was really scared. Anything could have happened. I never again trusted her out like that."

"I would think not."

"Anyway, it was odd, but about six months later, when I was putting in the stockade fence at the corner of the backyard, I stepped on something hard. It was the property marker under the leaves. For awhile I just kept putting in the fence. Then, I don't know why, but I stood at the marker and sighted the property line as it would cross the front sidewalk. And then I realized that Helga had stopped the neighbors exactly at where the property line would cross the sidewalk. And the weird thing is that in that area the next door driveway curves and there's a side embankment, an old iron gate, a leaning tree and our own sloping ground. So, there's no way to tell where our property ends and the neighbor's begins."

"Uh, yeah, that's strange. I've heard stories like that before." And then looking at me curiously, she asked, "Why do you say *our* property? Do you have another owner?"

"No," I said. "I just meant all of us. Helga and Raggie and Sono."

"Oh. Okay." Her eyes went to Helga. "She's certainly a wonderful dog."

"Yes. But she is sad, melancholy."

Then she said, "You've got so many trees here."

"Yeah. But too much shade for the grass to grow in the backyard here."

"Trees are important. I grew up with a lot of trees around."

"Doylestown."

"Right."

"I grew up with trees, too, in Florida. We had tons of trees in Jacksonville. I loved climbing them. Did you climb trees?"

"Oh, I played at it," she said dreamily. "Some people climb trees to conquer them, I think."

"Well, I'm not a conqueror. I think I just wanted to get away from things."

She rolled her eyes. "I can see that."

"So, what do you like about trees?"

Lifting her glass briefly and then returning it to the wet ring, she replied, "Maybe the oxygen."

Chapter 6

Turning my head afforded glimpses of her hands as she navigated the eastbound Schuylkill Expressway. "You okay?" I asked.

"Yes. Why?"

"Your hands seem tight on the wheel."

She loosened her grip. "Yeah, I guess so. I hate this drive."

"Driving's not a problem for you, though. I mean, I can see you handle a car pretty well."

"Think so?"

"It's obvious when someone hates the machine, as they say."

"Did you like driving?"

"I did, yeah. I was decidedly car oriented, growing up. My dad had a sports car. Stuff like that. Then I kind of grew away from it and just enjoyed driving."

"My dad liked cars, too. Mother would always say she'd rather he play with cars than women. . . . They fought, though."

"Don't they all?"

"Yes."

"So, you don't like driving the Schuylkill?"

"Oh God, no."

After crossing the city on the Vine Street Expressway, we left the car in a parking garage in Chinatown and took to the sidewalks to make our way back toward 12th Street. Under the clear sky the pavements radiated a luxurious heat that perhaps slowed our pace. Yes, it was a clear sky, one that seemed to promise everything. I thought of Thor, who had eaten his dinner and curled up in his corner of the patio under an evening sky that also seemed to promise everything. But then the truck arrived and the noosed stick appeared and he was betrayed.

At a busy corner she said, "Watch the curb, Stanly."

"Yeah. I'll be fine. I see it, thanks."

"Here, take my arm."

I did, just above her elbow. "Thanks."

"And just cross with me, okay?"

"Okay," I answered.

Once inside the market, which was not the typical supermarket with aisles and shoppers with carts but a huge pavilion of many vendors, we moved slowly through the swarm of people. Often I was forced to walk behind her. Because of the poor lighting I lost track of her occasionally, but fortunately she sensed my difficulty and extended a hand back to guide me. At an Amish kitchen we ordered soup and sandwiches to go and then at the market's central dining area looked for a table. We were surprised to find one right away and settled down for lunch.

"Crowded." I remarked, stirring my soup.

"Yep, always on Saturdays. But it's a great place. I love shopping here."

"You really know how to find the empty tables."

"Well, I'm not blind. God, I hate blind people."

"I guess that means me."

"Yep. How's the soup?"

"Excellent. I've never had Amish soup that wasn't."

"I know," she said.

"So, what do you think, would you call this a romantic lunch?"

She stared at me. "I don't know," she replied and then blew softly across a spoonful of soup. "Jury's out, probably. Does it matter?"

"You're teasing."

"I am," she laughed.

Nodding secretively to indicate a youngish family squabbling at a nearby table, I lowered my voice. "Would you call that an example of domesticity?"

For a moment she watched the husband and wife arguing, then replied, "Yes, but it's benign, obviously. The trouble is, it never stays that way."

"The cells turn bad and things become malignant, huh?"

"Yep."

"Always?"

"Seems that way. I wish I could say I've seen at least one happy marriage in my life, but I can't, I'm afraid."

"Sounds like the jury's in on that one. But I guess everybody keeps hoping."

She smiled. "Every generation, it seems, don't you think so?"

I did not respond.

Then she said, "Your eyes are pretty bad in here, aren't they?"

"Eye," I corrected.

"Vision. Your vision's bad in this light, isn't it?"

I pushed the straw to the bottom of my drink and shrugged.

"Can you see my green eyes?" she asked.

"Not really," I replied.

"Can you see my face?"

"Not very well."

She grew quiet, so I said nothing. The din of the chatter of the people around us became more pronounced, but just as it began to close in she asked, "So, why Black Moshannon?"

"What?"

"What made you pick Black Moshannon as a subject for your landscapes?"

"Uh, well, I don't know," I replied sluggishly. "I kind of fell in love with the place, I guess, the first time I saw it, really. I had gone there to camp. Everything was beautiful, and I set up the tent and went to sleep. The next morning, the weather was still beautiful, so I walked down to the lake and then to the bogs, took a look at everything, and it was all over, a done deal. Places, scenes, images, are like that, at least for me, either they work or they don't. And you don't know why."

"Like people. Relationships."

"Yes," I answered, "like relationships. Have you been to Black Moshannon?"

"I've heard of it. It's a state park, right?"

I nodded. "It's out near State College, about a five-hour drive from here. Kind of secluded and really natural. They seemed to leave the mosquitoes to the bats, that kind of thing."

"Did you go to hunt?"

"No - just camped. It was more than ten years ago. I was looking for new places to paint."

"But, *do* you hunt?"

I tried in vain to see her lips. "No," I answered. "I've never hunted. I could never do that, except for food, maybe, if I had to."

"Not for sport?"

"No."

Then she said, "I liked your abstracts too."

After a moment I said, "I'm sorry - my studio was really dirty."

She shook her head. "No, it was okay."

"I've been told my stuff's depressing."

A slow nod. "I guess I can see that about the drawings—yeah, I can see that. And maybe the scratchy paintings. But I loved the landscapes and seascapes, and I thought the nudes were exquisite. Actually, they surprised me."

"Which?"

"The nudes."

"Surprised you?"

"I don't know. I was glad they weren't exploitative."

"Glamorous?"

Again a nod, with a wave of her hand. "Sort of–"

"Sexy?"

"Well, I guess they were sexy, but I was glad you hadn't made the women vulnerable."

"You thought I'd do that?"

She smiled. "Some men would. There's nothing wrong with it. That's just the way a lot of men see women, or want to see them."

"So, that's back to the science?"

"Probably," she answered, her voice softened. Then she was silent.

All around us people were eating and talking, coming and going. Both the static and the moving were faceless, as though they were meaningless. I thought of Thor and of his loneliness as a misfit, and of how I had been the instrument of his destruction. It was true that I had commended him on the form I signed for the driver, writing in large print, "good dog—just can't keep him." But I knew this would do him no good at all, once they discovered his aggressive temperament. I could have kept him. I could have made it work. I could have left him inside during the day and then walked him on a leash when I came home. I could have gotten him a muzzle or done something else, anything to make it work so that the little neighbor girls would not be afraid of him. I could have given it more thought.

"You have it again," she said.

"What?"

"The sad face. You have the really sad face again."

I looked across at her, wishing with all my mind to clear the image and see the detail of its beauty. Keenly aware that I was actually being denied this wish, I simply averted my gaze, replying, "Sorry."

Then she said, "So, I'm talking to you and you're talking to me?"

"I'm sorry," I repeated. "Yes, I think that's what we're doing."

She gave a little sigh, almost not a sigh. Briefly she put her hand upon mine on the table, then withdrew it and said, "I don't know. I'm just thinking, asking myself about all this, what I'm doing."

Under the weight of a sense of helplessness, I offered, "Maybe, you're just talking to me and finishing your lunch. And then we'll do your shopping and just go from there." But even as I spoke the words the weight became heavier until it seemed unbearable.

"Yes. I'm shopping," she said reassuringly, as if speaking to herself as well as to me. "I'm doing my weekly shopping and you are with me."

"Yes."

"But that's what I want to know, why you are with me."

"You asked me to come along," I responded, and then, utterly helplessly, "It's just worked out this way, isn't that right?"

Soberly she replied, "I am your doctor. You are my patient."

At length I said, "That's not the problem, is it?"

"No," she answered, "I think not."

"The real problem is that I'm twice your age. I'm almost blind and soon will be. And I'm sick. I am sick, aren't I?"

She nodded. "Uh-huh. Yeah. You're pretty sick."

"In other words, I have no future to offer someone. At least, not a pleasant future." And when she didn't respond I said, "That's a nice dress. Is that called a flirty skirt?"

"Yes, it is. And it's not a dress, it's just a skirt. Top and skirt."

"Oh," I said quietly. "So, do you flirt in your skirt?"

"I have been known to, yes."

"But not much?"

"No," she replied. "Not very much." She looked down and then asked, "So, what, then, *are* we doing here together?"

"I don't know. You should know. A neurologist should know everything. What's the science say?"

"The science says it's chemistry. It says the mechanism's fairly complex but the reason is simple."

"And that's what you believe?"

She shrugged. "I'm a neurologist."

"And I'm a bad choice."

"Am I supposed to respond to that?"

"No," I answered. "No, you're not."

I knew it was useless. Dreams were like that, they were fantastic, and you were transient, and so was everyone else. At home the dogs would be resting, waiting for me to come back from this lunch and shopping. They would be getting their drinks of water and finding better places to curl up and wait for me.

"Could I ask you something?"

I looked up suddenly. "What?"

"Are you worried about something?"

I shook my head. "Not really."

"What were you thinking just now?"

"Just now?"

"Yes, just now," she insisted.

"I don't know. Just about the dogs."

"The dogs?"

"Yes, well, I was thinking that someone, anyone could break in and hurt them."

"There are three of them. That's, like, an army."

"I know."

"You're really security oriented, aren't you? Dogs, fences, locks. I mean, who's going to hurt your dogs? Like, think about it."

"But you have locks," I offered.

"Not like yours. I saw them. *Real* locks. And you checked them constantly to make sure they were locked."

"Uh, yes, I do that."

Again she put her hand upon mine. "You know, I think your dogs will be fine."

"I guess."

Then she lowered her voice. "See the dad?"

Discretely I looked toward the table with the squabbling family. I could see no details, but the husband, a toddler on his lap, seemed to be hustling to juggle things between two other children. His wife did not seem to be helping.

"Yes," I whispered to Roni. "He's pretty good. He's a busy guy."

"She's pregnant."

"Really?"

"Oh, yeah, *very*. See the milk shake?"

"No."

"Take my word for it. Anyway, my father was like that, family oriented. But I'm not sure I got his genes."

"Meaning?"

"Meaning I may be more a doctor than a mom."

"So, that's what we're doing here?"

She sighed again. "No, Stanly, I can't say that. I don't know what we're doing here."

I shook my head. "I don't either."

"But I don't think we're here simply as organisms at the end of a genetic chain."

"That's pretty mystical," I teased.

"It is." Then she said, "We should have had Chinese food. We could have read the fortunes."

"Yes."

The few times I saw her after that day were for office visits for quarterly checkups. She would be friendly, but only that, and her examination, as at the beginning, only perfunctory. She would ask about side effects of medicine and check for deterioration of muscle strength by having me grip her fingers. She would end with a look at my optic nerves, always placing one hand on my shoulder for stability as she came close with the instrument to look into my eye. When she made an entry in my chart or wrote a prescription for medicine or other labs I would gather from her face what images I could, trusting the brain to store the information for use at a future day when I might need to recognize her in a passing crowd.

The last time I saw her I sat in the chair while she silently read through her entries in my chart. At the end of the visit she looked directly at me and said, "I'm graduating. I'll be joining a practice near Doylestown."

"Oh," I said. "Okay. Well."

And then she asked, "How are your dogs?"

"They're fine, thanks."

"Helga?"

"Yes, fine," I replied. "Well, listen, maybe I'll see you sometime at the folk festival."

She nodded and lifted her chin just a little. "Yes. That would be great. I'll look for you."

As she shook my hand and smiled I looked for the last time into her green eyes.

BRENDA

Chapter 1

I first saw her as she stepped into the line queuing up for the 70 bus that ran from Fern Rock through East Oak Lane. I fell in behind her, only to have her suddenly turn half way around and speak.

"Hi," she said, keeping up with the line moving into the bus. "I've seen you and I've been meaning to say hi."

Her blond hair, which did not reach her shoulders, was striking in the five-thirty gloom, and I took a moment to enjoy it before replying.

"Yes, hi," I said and followed her up the steps. I slid my transit pass through the slot, listening for the beep, and then moved up beside her in the crowded aisle. Adjusting my shoulder bag, I looked again at the blond hair.

She smiled amiably. "I'm Brenda. Brenda Collins."

"Stanly Le Haley. Yes, hi."

"Do you work at the hospital?"

The bus began its movement nearly imperceptibly, but soon forced us to reach for the support rail.

"No, at the med school. You?"

"Infection control."

"Do you like the hospital?"

"What can I say? I'm a nurturer. I guess I need it."

I mentioned a few of the hospital people I knew, but she didn't know them. "Have you been there long?"

"No," she replied, giving her hair a shake. "A few months, actually. You?"

"Yes. A long time."

"What's a long time?"

"A little more than thirty years."

She raised her head in ascent. "Okay."

The contrast between the dark clip-on lenses, pale skin and blond hair was arresting. Yes, I had seen her before, but from a distance that melded her image into a benign blur. Here the image was neither blurry nor benign.

As we approached 5th we dropped into two vacated seats just in front of the back door. "I have to get off in a few blocks," I said.

"I know," she replied, adjusting the front of her trench coat. "By the reservoir."

Hiding my astonishment, for I had not seen her on the bus before, I remarked, "Cold front's coming in. You'll need a heavier coat tomorrow."

"Yes. You will, too. Snow, they say."

We fell silent as the bus turned at Godfrey and 5th and then made a stop at the exchange terminal not far from the intersection. Somehow the lapse from conversation seemed appropriate. It hadn't seemed to matter what we said, anyway. When the bus reached the reservoir she pulled the stop cord for me and said, "This is yours."

"Yes, thanks." I rose and adjusted my shoulder bag. "Listen, I'll see you. It was nice meeting you. Have a good evening."

"You too, thanks. See you."

Exiting at the back door, I turned to see her blurred, shadowy face in the window just before me and then the flat of her hand as she gave a quick wave. I returned the wave and watched as the bus pulled away.

The next morning a cold March wind blew into Philadelphia and blustered down Broad Street. At first it was steady, then hard and steady, and by noon it was pushing sleet. At three, heavy snow blew across the window of the fifth-floor stairwell, so that even I could see it. Thinking about the blond hair, I returned to my office. When the directory appeared on the screen under the flat magnifier, I clicked in the search box and typed her name.

The sleet and snow were strong as I stepped into the sheltered area just in front of the sliding doors of the hospital's main entrance. I pressed the Time button on my talking watch and then held the unit closer to my ear as the electronic female voice eerily announced that it was four-thirty. Then I saw Brenda's dark glasses as she passed through the first set of doors and then the second. Once again I acknowledged to myself that resistance to the magic of blond hair and dark glasses was futile.

"Hi," she said.

"Hi. Looks pretty bad, don't you think?"

"I suppose." She was clearly unimpressed with the blowing sleet. "Thanks for calling. You surprised me."

"Really?"

"I didn't anticipate it. Thanks."

"Sure. I just thought we could walk together." And turning I said, "Hey, look at the snow."

She gave me a scrutinizing look. "Well, it's good you wore a heavy coat."

"Yeah. And you did, too." And after a moment I said, "Okay. Well, here, why don't you take my arm."

With our free arms we braced her frayed umbrella before us and walked against the driving sleet. Somehow it was fun, and we laughed as we slogged along. We joked and said trivial things. Beside us the traffic crept away from the city. People had left early and their cars were clogging the city's exits. After two blocks we cautiously descended the sleet-strewn steps of the subway station. As she brushed the ice particles from her hair with a gloved hand, I closed the umbrella.

"It might be time for a new one," I said.

"Oh, yeah. That one's done."

On Monday we began to email each other and soon, depending on office workload, found ourselves conversing that way throughout the day. The well wishes for the day turned to questions about each other's background. She was Catholic, I was Christian but refused subgroup labels. She was born in the Year of the Horse, I the Year of the Rat. Her sign was Aquarius, mine Leo. She grew up in Philadelphia, I in Jacksonville, Florida. She had expected to become a nun, I a monk.

Soon we began meeting for lunch once a week, then twice a week. We exchanged movies. She brought films like *Dave* and *Whale Rider*. I brought films like *White Fang* and *Two Brothers*.

On a bright day in May we sat upon a low wall by the hospital, content from a hearty Chinese takeout lunch and nearly dreamy with the beautiful weather. Beyond the sidewalk the traffic streamed.

"Time's on our side today," she said, looking at her watch.

"Yeah. Looks good."

"You know," she said, gazing at the traffic, "Horses are supposed to be totally incompatible with Rats."

"Yes," I chuckled. "I know. Too bad."

"Those things aren't that accurate, though."

"No," I said. "I have read that the Chinese sometimes use their astrology as a social tool. Instead of asking someone's age, which would be rude, they ask the sign. Since the recurrence of a sign is only every twelve years, the age can usually be guessed."

"Zodiacs are interesting."

"Everything's interesting."

She looked at me. "You're in an agreeable mood."

"I suppose."

"Have you done any astrology art?"

"I have a painting called *Golden Sky—Year of the Dragon* and maybe a couple others."

"Does it have a dragon in it?"

"Recognizable? No," I said, watching a passing bus, "not really. It started out with one, but it got sort of developed out."

"What're you doing this afternoon?"

"Setting up a manuscript. You?"

"Nothing much," she said. "So, are you writing a book?"

"What makes you ask?"

She lifted her eyebrows. "Curious."

"Actually, I was once told that I should never become a writer because I had no powers of observation. What can I say? I think they were kind of right. Anyway, no. No book."

"Never?"

"I wouldn't say that."

"Good," she said. "Maybe someday."

"Possibly. If I do write one, I'll probably put you in it. What do you think?"

"Why me?"

"I don't know. Maybe because you don't really add up. Plus, you have a colorful background."

"What doesn't add up?"

"All the things you told me. I don't know. Being a wild kid. Not finishing high school. A strict mother. A father you hardly knew and now seem reluctant to acknowledge. Runaway marriage at, what, sixteen? Losing your baby. The beatings. Divorce. Then living with the older guy and riding around on the back of his motorcycle, still just a kid dreaming of the universe." I chuckled, and then we both did. "Then another marriage. Friday nights going from bar to bar. Another divorce. And then, deciding out of nowhere to enter night school and get a degree. And you actually do it, you stick to it and achieve it, and you do this in your forties. Now you're an administrative assistant at a major hospital. No, you don't add up. Most people don't emerge so successfully from a background like that."

Staring at me, she said, "I don't have perfect grammar."

I shrugged. "It's pretty good, let me tell you. You're well spoken, you're nice to look at, and you have your degree. I can't believe doors won't open for you."

After a moment she said, "You think I'm nice to look at?"

"Yes, I do. And you come across as professional, more like an administrator than administrative assistant."

"You see me as an administrator?"

I nodded. "I think so. Did you have any business courses? I think you have to have a pretty good sense of business to be an administrator."

"I'm more a people person."

"But no business courses?"

"Not really. I've been thinking of doing a master's in some kind of arbitration. I suppose I'm a real Aquarian."

"Water Bearer, huh?"

Her gaze returned to the traffic. "As an administrator I'd be thinking more about the people than the system."

"Democrat, huh?"

She gave a single nod and answered sincerely, "Oh, yeah." And then, with obvious scrutiny, she asked, "What are you, a Republican?"

"Neither."

"An Independent?"

"No. I think I'm a little of all three. And more of some other things."

Eyeing me, she said, "You're a Communist? I thought Communism was dead. What *are* you?"

"Why do I have to be any of them?"

Holding both hands apart, as if to show the distance between them, she said emphatically, "You have to pick *something*."

"Why?"

"Because it only makes sense. That's why the systems are there."

"I think they all just represent facets of human thinking. They're methods for solving problems. I think Russia needed what it needed in 1917, China needed what it needed in 1948, and America needed what it needed when it formed itself."

"You don't think everybody should be free?"

"Not if they don't want to be. The people always have the power to be what they want."

"So, you're really into politics?" she asked.

"Not really."

"You're just a realist, right?"

"I guess I'm a realist, a romanticist and an idealist. A bit of all three. Which I suppose makes me nothing."

"Yeah. Why do you have to be any of them, right? Just be nothing."

"I suppose."

"Oh, man. I think you're a can of worms. And I'll bet there's a lot of worms in there."

"Well, then maybe we should both just write books."

Shaking her head, she said, "I think you should just be quiet."

So, I was quiet and let the blue of her dress entertain me as I waited for her to say something else.

"Better get back," she said, looking at her watch.

"Yeah, I think so."

"Don't want to be late."

"No," I said.

"So, why are you almost blind?"

"MS."

With a tone that suggested I might have mentioned it earlier, she said, "You have MS?"

"Uh-huh."

After a moment she said, "I worked with MS patients once. Some were bed ridden. Not good."

"Well, that might have been the Progressive form. Mine's what they call Relapsing-Remitting, because there's remission after an attack. With Progressive the attack is just kind of steady. Mine can turn to Progressive, but maybe it won't. Actually, a pretty high percentage of the Relapsing people eventually move into the Progressive category, but I haven't yet."

"So, yours isn't as bad?"

"No. I mean, it's still bad. With MS your body is basically attacking its own cells." I shrugged. "It destroys your nervous system. In an attack the sheath around nerves is inflamed, and after the attack is left scarred. It's like having bad wiring, you're constantly short circuiting. Sometimes, like with me, the optic nerves are involved. It can blind you."

"What's it like?"

"Well, I'm on interferon, and that minimizes the attacks. Attacks for me were incredible, just really indescribable. And then I'm on an immunomodulator, which basically keeps the inflammation away from the optic nerve."

"So, you don't feel anything?"

"Well, yeah, you still feel sick, a combination of unwellness and fatigue just about all the time."

"It leaves you scarred?"

"Your nerves, yeah."

She was quiet. Finally she remarked, "You know, I never thought your vision was bad until you told me."

"I try to work around it. You get used to it. It's not so bad."

"You said you're legally blind?"

"Uh-huh."

"Got a good doctor?"

"He seems to be very good, yeah."

"Here?"

"No."

She glanced at her watch again. "Come on, let's go back."

When we parted at the hospital I watched her pass through the sliding doors and then meld with the crowd. She had an aloneness about her, and the sense of this aloneness stayed with me as I crossed the street and returned to the medical school.

In my office I pressed the water boiler's left button, spooned loose oolong into my cup, and placed two fig bars on a section cut from a paper towel. As the boiler began to hiss I sat down at the computer and peered absentmindedly through the magnifier. As the boiler finished and clicked off I became aware of new tingling in my hands and forearms. I flexed my fingers and felt my forearms. Both arms were slightly numb from elbow to finger tips. When I had filled the cup I opened my email and then a new message from Brenda. Expanding the font, I read, *Hi. Lunch was nice. I had a good time. Thanks for all the info. Life is filled with strange dreams, isn't it?*

Reclining as far as possible in the old typing chair, I thought of the hair, the sunglasses, the dress, the whole image as she had sat in the sunlight and talked. And I thought of her aloneness. I imagined her in her youth moving with the rhythm of the motorcycle as she was being wheeled around the neighborhoods. Strange dreams.

Chapter 2

As I pulled the magnum from the top shelf of the metal cabinet I could nearly feel the paintings behind me, landscapes of Black Moshannon, seascapes of Cape May, and spatial, linear and symbolic abstracts. Oils, acrylics, pen-and-inks, photographs. I locked the cabinet, slid the inside-the-pants holster a little farther back until the rig was comfortable, and turned around to consider the draft on the easel. Switching on the two side lamps that hung from the main fluorescent light over the easel, I stepped closer. How had it seemed so perfect last night? And where did all the white come from? It looked more like a snow scene than a bog. Oh, nothing wrong with the linear aspects, as I could still see to draw. But the rest of it, what a mess. Recalling Roni's suggestion to go linear instead of trying to do what I could no longer do, I switched off the lights and left the studio.

When I reached the kitchen, Ragnar, Sono, and Tai Ping, who had spent their usual half hour chasing each other and racing through the yard while I changed clothes after coming home from work, were frantically clawing at the back door to be let in. When I reached the landing to the basement they stopped clawing and waited for me to flip the hook lock and throw open the door. Then as I stood aside they blew past me en masse, leaped up the short steps, and filled the kitchen with a theatrical display of gladiatorial combat. It was all part of the workday evening routine. They seemed never to tire of it, but only to grow keener to participate in its pattern, and while I mixed the wet and dry food in their bowls they pushed me with their noses and snarled at each other playfully. Then when I held the bowls aloft, first for Raggie and Sono and then for Tai Ping, they snapped into sitting position and froze there with glittering eyes until the bowls were lowered to the floor.

It was always a joy for me to watch them eat. To hear the slobbering and wolfing and then to see each of them, just after they were finished, lick the other bowls somehow gave me a sense of satisfaction. They were fast eaters, so by the time I had wiped the table they were already starting to lick the other bowls. And then, as always, I gave them each a hug. "Okay, okay." I said. "Rough dogs. Oh, who needs a hug? I don't know. Two wolves and a gladiator, I think. Now, who wants to go outside?" More inspired than energized by their dinner, they scrambled down the short steps and then burst out into the yard as I pushed the door open again.

As it was an interferon night, I clicked the button on the old CD player and retrieved the box of injections from the refrigerator. Then, after peeling down one side of an alcohol swab, I sat at the table to listen to the opening of Bruckner's seventh. And who would not stop for a moment to listen to that opening? The countless times I had followed its development had served to make it just one more pattern my memory could rely upon. I thought of Brenda's face and how during a conversation at one of our lunches I had guessed her ethnicity. "You have a wonderful East European face," I had said. But why had she been defensive when I guessed, more specifically, Polish and Irish? "You are very close," she had replied, somewhat perturbed. "My mother is Lithuanian, and my father, Irish."

I was just finishing with the injection, when the phone rang. Returning the used needle to its plastic sleeve, I dropped it into the sharps container, pulled up my jeans, and reached for the receiver. I was surprised to hear Brenda's voice. In twenty minutes she was at the door. Usually the presence of anyone on the other side of the Plexiglas drove the dogs into a frenzy, but for some reason Brenda's smiling face invoked no response from them. She had not met them before but only seen them in the yard as she occasionally passed the house. As she stepped inside the enclosed porch she greeted each dog by name.

I was amazed. "How did you know their names?"

"Oh, give me a break," she said. "You've talked about them enough."

As they circled her I warned, "Don't touch them yet. Just let them sniff. They're inspecting you."

"They look a little dangerous. I've seen them in the yard sometimes."

"They seem to like you. It's pretty obvious when they don't. Just put your packages on the radiator cover there. It looks like wine."

"Of course. But nonalcoholic, just for you. The other one's bread. Figured you might not have any."

"Oh?"

She threw me a cryptic look. "Experience."

I reached for the packages and we left the porch. The dogs still circled and sniffed. Poor Ragnar, who, I was convinced, could not be socialized, hung her head and presented an unmistakable aura of unhappiness. In the foyer Brenda stopped and turned toward the living room. I could see she was looking at the paintings and I hoped she would not say something terribly stupid. For a moment she didn't say anything. Neither did I. I could not be certain in the dim lighting of the foyer, but she seemed to be smiling.

Then she asked, "New?"

"Uh, no, not really. Actually I change them a lot."

"They're nice. I'll have to take a closer look."

"Sure. I put them up for all kinds of reasons. New ones, to think about them, see if they're finished or not. And older ones, I suppose, to inspire me."

"Inspire you?"

"Yeah, well, I kind of live in the past. So, when I see things I did years ago, I get new ideas. Sometimes."

She nodded. "I do that a lot. Old clothes."

In the kitchen I took the bottle from the paper bag and put it in the refrigerator. "Is that okay?"

"Oh, sure. Whatever," she said, pushing a kitchen chair closer to the table. "Here. Give me the bread. I'll cut it. Do you have a cutting board?" Glancing around casually, she said. "So, you weren't going to invite me?"

I scratched the underside of my beard. "Maybe I'm shy."

"Right. I've had guys say that before."

"Plural?"

"Yes. Plural. Does it matter?"

"No." I shook my head. "Actually, I don't really entertain. I'm not good at it. So."

"Okay. Well, maybe I can help."

"I was going to make spaghetti. Is that okay?"

"Perfect. Good." Then with both hands she ran her fingers through her hair to smooth it back. It was a practice people usually left in their youth.

"You know, you do that."

"What?"

"Smooth your hair back that way."

"How?"

"Like you just took your helmet off."

"You notice a lot, for somebody who's not supposed to be observant."

"Sometimes," I replied.

It was half an hour later that I turned the cold tap on full and drained the boiling water from the pasta. It was the kind of task that low vision had turned into a challenge for me. When the water seemed to have completely drained I set the covered pot beside the plates on the table. Somehow the paisley tablecloth, which she had insisted on bringing from its home in a drawer, decorated with proper settings of plates, glasses, knives, forks and spoons, made me stop. Looking at the individual bowls of steaming corn and peas she had prepared, I said, "Should I put this in a bowl or something? Pot seems a little crass."

"Oh, that's fine," she replied.

"What's fine? Putting it in a bowl?"

"No, the pot. The pot's fine."

"Okay," I said, perhaps a little relieved. "Hey, the table looks great. Thanks. I don't usually eat with a tablecloth."

"I can see why," she said, glancing toward the dogs, who lay asleep on the old carpet in the adjacent breakfast room.

"Oh, the dogs? Yeah, they're a little rough. Ping's a brute. He's up on the table half the time."

She straightened a knife at a place setting. "This is a great old house. Kind of big. It's all yours?"

I adjusted my sleeve. "Yep. Theirs and mine."

She gave a short laugh toward Tai Ping, who was sprawled across the doorway into the kitchen. "Yours and the dogs', huh?"

"Uh-huh."

"You think dogs should own things?"

I tilted my head slightly to one side. "Uh-huh. Shall we sit down? Are we ready to eat?"

"Yeah, sure. Perfect."

"I have grape juice and soda."

"No wine?"

"Oh. Yeah. Sorry. And you have the glasses out too."

When we had poured the wine and settled in for the meal, I bowed my head and silently gave thanks.

"Amen and amen," she said.

"You always say that."

"Yes," she chuckled. "I tease."

"Not unpleasantly," I remarked, picking up my wine glass.

"You said you had preached. How long? Were you a minister?"

"No, not a minister. I was in a Plymouth Brethren assembly for about nine years. They didn't have ministers, just elders. I wasn't an elder. I ended up speaking a lot, because people seemed to like what I had to say. But the elders didn't. And I'm sure, to them, my views seemed more than a little wacky. It just didn't work out." Passing the bread to her, I said, "The wine's good. Thanks."

"Sure."

"And the bread looks great. I didn't know I had so many bowls."

Pleased, she said, "Sometimes I take groceries to the convent. There aren't many of them left. They're completely cloistered, so you can see them only on a little closed-circuit monitor. They sell sacred medals and things."

"Groceries?"

"They're very poor. People take them things."

"So, would you say that's the Catholic or the Aquarian in you?"

She hesitated. "I don't know. The Catholic, I presume. Are you guilt-driven?"

"I'm afraid so," I admitted.

"Then you're Catholic." Then she chuckled. "Too bad. Guilt can give you scars deeper than the optic nerves." When I did not reply she asked, "So, did you read about that spy?"

"Uh-huh, I did. Do you think Putin killed him?"

She hesitated. "I don't know. Maybe. That's what they say. Who else could have done it?"

With my fork I twirled pasta in the meatless sauce, which seemed a worthy ritual. "Do you think he was right?"

"Putin?" she shot back. "I hope they catch him and lock him up." And then quite deliberately, "Don't you?"

"We're never going to know enough of the story to be satisfied."

"But if he ordered the guy poisoned? If we actually find it out?"

With my fork and a piece of bread I collected the last of my spaghetti. "That's the spy world. The guy had no business going to the West and blabbing about the KGB, or whatever he did. But then, how can we know what motivated him? Maybe he had a good reason. But motive aside, he was dangerously provoking a wolf."

"But it was murder," she said and then waited for an answer.

I shook my head and swallowed, reaching for my glass. "Not in that world. I don't think so. If one of our guys went over there and started blabbing about the CIA, we'd probably do the same thing. Maybe in a different way, but we'd do the same thing. And for good reason. That's a pretty secret world. It has to be." As I watched her raise her glass to her lips, I was grateful for the residual acuity in my right eye. I watched her swallow the wine and wondered what she had looked like at eighteen. I wondered too why she had been vague in her answers to my questions about her past. Why she had said she used various last names in her youth but then had declined to divulge what they were. Why she had claimed there were no photographs from her youth. I had searched the internet in vain for information about her. Even her high school web site had yielded nothing.

"It's too bad you can't have real wine," she said.

"Yes, I know," I said. "Wine's good. Actually, I really like scotch. With ice. But they said no alcohol, even in cake. The meds are kind of tough on the liver." Under the table Sono brushed my leg, and I reached to touch her thick coat as she passed. I knew she was looking for a different spot. Tai Ping and Ragnar were still asleep.

"Have you always liked dogs?"

I lifted my hands a little but didn't reply.

"Are they always this quiet?"

"No, actually they're not," I said. "They're passive tonight. I don't entertain much."

"I gathered that," she said.

"Ah. Sarcasm?"

"No, just a tease."

"Do you entertain?"

"Not much. My sisters sometimes. And I have a few girlfriends from when I lived in Olney. I'll meet them for dinner and we'll go back to my apartment to watch a movie and talk. Just catch up on stuff. I like having people over, but after work I usually just want to crash. And cleaning's a pain." She threw a glance toward the stove.

"No men?"

"Sometimes." There was something in her voice that told me she wanted me to have this information. "So, are you doing any writing?"

"I told you, I'm not observant."

"Right."

"What do you think I should write?"

"I thought you might've already started a story or novel. You've asked me enough about myself to fill a book."

"I don't know," I said. "I can finish a poem but not a piece of prose. I make periodic attempts at short stories and novels, but never seem to get anywhere. The problems are chronic. You know, doubt, lack of direction."

Sensing the meal was over, the dogs roused themselves and took up positions beside my chair.

"What do they want? Scraps?"

"Well, not exactly," I replied. "They always help me finish my meal." I reached for the pot and dumped the rest of the pasta on my plate. Mixing it with the sauce remaining on my plate, I held the first batch to Tai Ping's mouth. Instantly his huge mouth opened and closed on my fingers to take the spaghetti.

"Oh, good grief. Do they ever bite you?"

"Not really. At least, they don't mean to."

As I began to feed them buttered pieces of the bread she asked, "Don't they say not to feed dogs from the table?"

"Yes, they do. I've heard that. And I've read it, too. Yes."

"Is it sanitary?"

"Probably not," I admitted as Sono took a piece of bread from my fingers. "Why don't you start a book yourself? You're the one with the colorful life. I mean, why not try? You're well spoken. Just put your thoughts down."

She seemed pleased but was quiet at this. She pushed her hair back again with both hands, and I hoped she would stay for the evening. And then, rather oddly, we arose at the same time, cleared the table, stacked the dirty dishes by the dishwasher, and wiped the counters, as if preparing for some domestic event. But what event could there be? And what reason could there be for preparing for it? To invest in relationships? To strengthen security? To be able to spend time in peace watching the sun go up and down?

"You know," she said as I began to fill the kettle for tea, "I'd love to have a tour, if a certain man would like to show me around."

"Oh, sure," I said, parking the kettle on the stove. "Okay, I'll be your tour guide. What would you like to see first? You've seen most of the downstairs."

She folded her dishtowel and draped it over its rack. "Hey, show me everything. I'd like to see it all, if that's okay."

"Even the laundry room?"

"Why not? That'd be fun."

"Okay," I said cheerfully. "Well, let's grab a couple flashlights. We'll need them."

"What?"

I chuckled. "Just kidding. Come on."

Flipping the switch to the basement lights, I led with the dogs down to the laundry room. I looked on curiously as she gave the place a quick examination. She did not seem interested in the two piles of dirty clothes, but neither did she miss them.

"I can run the washer for you, if you like," I said.

"Oh, don't be a drip," she shot back. "What's over there?"

"Work bench and tools. Here, come on."

"You fix things?" she asked, following me.

I switched on the overheads, lighting up the work area. "Sure. I do my own house repairs, except for major things, like replacing the heater, which needs to be done soon, I think. I put in the whole kitchen. It was a mess when I moved in."

"You did everything?"

Yes. Cabinets, sink, garbage disposal, dishwasher, stove, lighting. I had to move a gas line for the stove and install a new electric line for the dishwasher, but it wasn't difficult."

"You're an electrician?"

"Not really. I just sort of taught myself everything."

"Well, the kitchen was beautiful. You do nice work."

"Thanks," I replied. "See, the whole basement is one big room. That's my bike over by the oil tank. I used to ride to work."

"In the city? Dangerous."

"Actually, yes, it was. I rode year around for about twelve years. Not now, of course."

"Oh, your vision, yeah."

"Vision and MS."

"But you can still do house repairs?"

"Sure. I have to be careful with power tools. The most difficult thing now is working with wiring. I've replaced nearly all the electric lines in the house, but still I have to rewire a box now and then, and it's really hard to see what I'm doing. But I've worked through it so far. I try to be careful. Come on, I'll show you the other floors."

At the first-floor level I led her from the kitchen to the dining room. Switching on the ceiling light, I said, "I don't dine in here, so I think of this as my relaxation room. It's where I watch movies, do my studies, and just relax with the dogs."

"I can believe that. It smells a little more doggy in here. That's an old couch. It looks comfortable." Picking up a three-dimensional cube puzzle, she remarked, "You like puzzles. I saw two others in the living room when I came in."

"You're a detective."

She set the puzzle down. "I think I'd want to relax in here, too. It's peaceful. Your dogs must love this rug."

"Yes, they do. I should vacuum it sometime."

She gave me an odd look and then said, "Okay. How about the second floor?"

On the upstairs landing she requested to use the bathroom, so I went with the dogs to wait in the front bedroom. I didn't bother to pick things up, as she seemed curious as to how I lived. When she came in she stood quietly and then politely remarked that I seemed organized. Then, after showing her the middle room, which I used mainly for storing paintings and frames and where Sono slept on a single bed, I led her to the third-floor attic. Finished by the previous owner, the spacious attic had its own bathroom and two bedrooms, which I used as a library and a storage room. Finally, I led the five of us down to the second floor again and into the studio, where I switched on the overhead lights and pushed in the desk chair to make room for her.

"That's everything," I said. "And we end up here."

"That was a nice tour. Thank you."

"Sure."

"Is this enough space for you? The room seems completely full of paintings. And your desk is so big. And you have your computer here, too. How can you work?"

"I know," I replied, a little embarrassed. "It seems odd, I guess, to cram so much in here when the house is so big."

"Yes. Can you paint effectively in here? There's just no space left. Some of your canvases are large. How do you manage that?"

"With difficulty, actually." I lifted my shoulders in apology. "I don't know I haven't spread out more. Maybe it's fetal. I like things cozy."

"I guess you do. It's nice in here. I love the smells. It just *seems* like a studio."

After switching on the easel's side lamps and pushing the power button on the CD player's remote I had hot-glued to the winch block, I replied, "It gets really cramped with the dogs in here."

"The music's nice. What is it?"

"Etudes for ballet."

"I didn't know you liked piano music."

"Mostly symphonies. But yeah, piano's very beautiful. The dogs seem to like it."

Nodding slowly, she turned her attention to the paintings. Oddly, her interest persisted until she had seen nearly every piece in the studio, whether in draft stage or finished. She even asked to see the pen-and-inks. She had difficulty commenting on the aesthetics of any of the pieces, including the photographs, offering instead the wearisome statement I had heard from so many others, that she didn't know a lot about art but knew what she liked. At a technical level she was practically totally ignorant and could only comment that colors were bright or that paint was thick. I was okay with all of this; experience had taught me to be okay with it. But in the end, although I was glad she had not said grossly stupid things, I was disappointed that she had been unable to intelligently approach my art aesthetically or technically.

I resorted to small talk. "So, how do I live? What are your findings?"

"What?"

"You've been scrutinizing me, right?"

"Somewhat, I suppose. Women do that."

"Do they? So, women do certain things and men do certain things?"

"I'm not entirely new school."

"So, what have you seen?"

"Oh, nothing too bad," she said. "You know, you must have a puzzle in every room."

"I like puzzles."

"I guess so."

"What else," I asked, amused.

"There's not a curtain in this house. And I don't mean to be critical, but you need someone to clean. You have dirty floors, sir." She shook her head. "Sorry. But you do."

"Yeah. No, I think you're right. But they don't seem to mind."

"Who?"

"The dogs," I replied, switching off the CD player.

For the rest of the evening we sat on the living room couch, the dogs at our feet, and drank tea and ate fig bars and talked. I apologized for not having herb tea, for not bringing the tea on a tray, and for not having pastry. But none of those things seemed to matter.

"I was going to get a digital camera," she said. "Do you think I should?"

"Yes. They're wonderful."

"I'm not really a photographer. It would just be to carry with me for taking spontaneous pictures. Was the one in your studio digital?"

"Yes, it was. I changed from film about a year ago. It's great to be able to do everything on the computer. It's liberating. Film was a mess."

After a moment she asked, "Are you all right? You don't look so good."

"I'm sorry," I said, shifting a little. "It's just the interferon."

"Oh."

"I'm okay."

She stared at me. "Maybe I should go."

"No, no. I'm fine, really. I take it every week. It's not a problem. Listen, would you like more tea?"

"No, I'm good."

"You know, I'm sort of socially inept. So, if you have to go, it's okay."

And then she relaxed. "No, I'm good."

"So," I said, probably laboriously, "tell me more about why you didn't become a nun."

She gave a short laugh. "Oh boy, probing again. You've gotta be writing that book. I told you. There's nothing more to tell. It didn't work out. Maybe like your preaching. I don't know. Life turned a corners and I went with it. I complained, but I was glad too. It was a nebulous time for me. Now I'm too old."

Suddenly a streak of pain ran down my right side, causing me to wince. Startled, she asked, "Are you okay? What was that?"

"A shock. I'm okay."

"What kind of shock?"

"An electric shock. You get them, sometimes, with MS."

"Do they hurt?"

"Mostly just annoying," I replied. "Why is fifty-three too old to become a nun? That's not too old. Lots of people do it."

"That's great cheerleading. But lots of people *don't* do it. Nobody wants to be a nun these days." She was quiet for a moment and then said, "I think I liked men too much, to go into a convent. I would have gone crazy as a nun. And the isolation. I don't know."

"Isolation doesn't bother me," I said. "I kind of prefer it."

She grinned. "As in, the more people you meet, the more you like your dogs?"

"Maybe a little."

"Are you suicidal at all? I read about your medicine. It can make you suicidal."

"I know. I've been warned. Yeah, it can do that. No, I'm okay. I'm fine. Some of the side-effects can be annoying, but compared to steroids, interferon's a whiz."

"That's funny. People don't say that anymore."

"What? *Whiz*? Yeah. Kind of dates me."

"I wonder what things I say that date me."

"So, are you suicidal?"

"No," she said, "not me."

"Catholics are really against it, right?"

"*Everybody's* against it."

"Not the people who do it." Then I asked, "What about assisted suicide?"

She was clearly peeved, but replied, "I suppose it's okay, if someone's in pain and can't get out of it."

Inexplicably, Tai Ping raised his head, Sono raised hers, and Ragnar raised hers. Then the three dogs arose at once, as if stirring for an unpleasant task. I marveled as I watched them. Their stretching and yawning seemed to announce that the evening should be coming to a close.

Without a word, we carried the tea things to the kitchen. She rinsed the cups and saucers while I let the dogs out.

"Can I help you with the dinner dishes?" she asked.

"No," I replied, "I'll be fine."

"Martyr?"

"No. Loading the dishwasher's pretty easy. But, thanks."

Raising one shoulder, she said, somewhat awkwardly, "Well, listen, thanks for having me."

"Sure. Thanks for coming. I had a good time."

She blinked once and said, "So did I."

"I'll walk you home. You're close by, right?"

"What about your vision?"

"I'm okay on the sidewalk. I'll be fine. Let me get them in."

After letting the dogs in, I gave them each a biscuit and checked the water bowl. While Brenda was in the bathroom I returned the magnum to the gun cabinet, secured the back door, and checked the windows.

When she returned I said, "Let me get the wine. There's a lot left. It was very good."

"Oh, no, that's for you. My apology gift for inviting myself."

"Thank you. I'll have it in the evenings."

"Don't get drunk," she teased.

I replied, "That would be a trick."

Before closing the front door I gave Tai Ping, Ragnar and Sono each a hug and then locked them in. "I'll be back," I said to them. "Not long."

At the front sidewalk she said, "You leave the lights on?"

"I think the dogs are safer that way."

"Safer?"

"Yeah. I think so."

She was incredulous. "They're fierce!"

"Yeah. They're pretty serious."

"And two of them are wolves."

"No, they just look like it."

The nighttime air felt luxurious in my lungs, but the sidewalk had turned into a dark tunnel. I stepped higher than I usually did, to avoid the jutting slabs I knew must be there. There was supposed to be a moon out, but I knew that moonlight no longer helped.

At the first corner she warned, "Watch the curb."

"Right. Thanks. The streetlights are playing games with me, I think."

At the third corner she said, "A lira for your thoughts."

"You might want your money back."

"It's my money."

But I was silent. There seemed nothing to say. Half a block farther, we stopped in front of an old house similar to mine. It was all very dark and quiet, with a single window glowing and a tiny light on the open porch near the front door.

"My apartment's at the back, on the second floor," she said. "But I go in at the front door. I'm sure my landlady's asleep by now."

"This is about like mine," I said. "At least what I can see of it."

"I was thinking that."

"East Oak Lane has hundreds of these old houses. Stone foundation, leaky basement, squirrels in the attic, tons of space."

"And charming."

"Yes. Charming." I was disappointed that I could not see more of her hair in the darkness.

"Well, listen," she said, almost shyly, "I do have to go in. Thanks again."

"Yes. Thanks for coming over. I'll wait till you get in."

She took a few steps and then asked, "Will you be okay getting back?"

"Yes. I'll be fine. Good night."

"Good night."

When the door closed behind her, I turned and walked toward home. Again the streetlights played their games, and I stepped even higher. Yes, there was supposed to be a moon out. I believed the moon was up there, but I was not romantic enough to believe it rode upon a cloud or watched over lovers.

Chapter 3

On a Monday morning in early June I sat at my computer at work and sipped tea and munched cookies before beginning the workday. The previous night's rain had left the air moist for my walk to the bus stop on the way into work, and there was still the sensation of it in my lungs and I relaxed in my chair. Dry air always made it more difficult for me to breathe. With another sip of tea in my mouth I sat up and opened my email, hoping for a message from Brenda. Nothing was there, so I clicked Compose and typed, *Good morning. How is the Aquarian this morning? What do you plan for today? I have your movie to return. Shall we meet after work? Have a good morning.*

Then I clicked Send and sat back again and thought about the dogs at home, what they might be doing or thinking as they began their day. Already I missed them. They were so good about holding their bladder each day until I got home, and when they couldn't, going in the basement so I could clean it up in the evening. As I wondered why they made this effort I recalled an incident I had witnessed in the city earlier that year. A man on a rickety bicycle, with his dog on a leash, was slowly riding across the crosswalk at the intersection of 17th and Spruce. In the middle of the crossing, with virtually no traffic to press the situation, the man apparently inadvertently let go of the leash. The dog, pathetically docile, simply stopped walking when the leash dropped beside him. Instantly the man stopped, too, and either from embarrassment, wickedness, or whatever, began to scream curses down at the dog, as if to demonstrate to any onlookers that the dog had pulled the leash free himself. From the way he hung his head, it seemed the dog was used to the vitriol that issued from the man's mouth. Dismounting the contraption, the man retrieved his end of the leash and gave it a horrendous yank. It was obvious from the poor dog's acceptance of this that he was used to physical abuse as well. I hadn't seen such things very often. But they invariably left me wondering why nature had been either configured or left to configure itself such that animals were subject to the brutality of humans, not just to their intelligence but to their evil. I found it incredible that dogs had a tendency to continue to serve and even protect those who mistreated them. It was true that women often interpreted a potential husband's treatment of animals as the way he would come to treat his family. But this was not enough, I wanted much more from nature, and if not from nature, from God. I could not help wishing that God would just stop and reconfigure the whole business so that nature would hold such retribution for human abuse of animals, especially the serving beasts, as to discourage even the boldest brute.

It was not until just after lunch that Brenda's answer came in. *Hi Stanly. Sorry I could not get back to you sooner. I was sent on an errand around the hospital. I am so busy! I like being busy but not frantic like this. I can't stand shit all over my desk! Gotta straighten it up. The Aquarian is good. How is the Leo? Okay let's meet up after work. I'll see you at the same place about 5. Will see you then. Brenda.*

Each day until Thursday afternoon her email message was short and somewhat frenetic. On Friday we met for lunch and walked to the Chinese take-out behind the hospital. The sky was quite dark, but the pavement was still dry when we took our lunches to the student/faculty center. Amid the sounds of a nearby game of ping pong we pulled up chairs to an isolated table and opened our bags.

"So, how's the translation coming," she asked.

"Okay."

"And what's *okay* mean?"

I shrugged. "I think I'll like the work."

"You haven't started?"

"I did a small section. That went well."

"Good. So, what's next?"

"I'm hesitating."

"Why not just start?"

"Because I failed the first time, like I told you."

"But that was fifteen years ago, you said. I mean, come on, be realistic. It's time to try again."

I waved a hand to the side. "Right. No, I'll try. I will. I'm starting with Philippians, I think."

"Can't wait to see it. Good luck."

For a few moments we sat, quietly enjoying the food. Then I asked, "Will it rain?"

"You won't melt," she retorted.

I hated clichés. I forced my response. "That's true." Looking across at her face, I wished for a narrower table so I might see the pale gray eyes.

She pushed her food with her fork. "They probably sell umbrellas here."

"Yes. So, what do you do when your hair gets wet?"

She looked at me. "You mean, from the rain?"

"Yeah. What do you do?"

"Just push it back and let it dry. Sometimes I dry it with a handkerchief."

"Is the shrimp and broccoli good?"

"It's okay." Then she said, "Why curious about my hair?"

"I don't know," I said. "I don't know."

She didn't press it, but I could see she was smiling. "What do you think about women being ordained as priests?"

"It's okay with me. It's only religion."

"Religion's important."

I sighed. "To some people."

"It's important to me."

At length I said, "Anyway, I think religion can be what you want it to be. And actually, that's all it can be. God doesn't seem to care. He seems to look beyond the religion to get to the faith. I think faith is God's idea for communicating with man, and religion is man's idea for communicating with God. So, I think religion's like the art of man's faith."

"You're not a friend of religion, are you?"

"I don't mind religion," I said, "as long as it's called that. But calling religion faith is a lie, or at least an error."

"Sounds like everything's a lie to you."

"Yeah, I guess I'm pretty cynical."

"Could you tell me something, why are you translating the New Testament?"

"Mainly to get rid of the religious terms."

"What terms?"

"Tons of them. Words like *holy*. It simply means *dedicated* or *set aside*, but *holy* is a religious word or at least has become one. Every translation's filled with religious terms. And I want to read it in its linguistically generic form. I don't like someone always telling me what something means, as if I'm too dumb to figure that out for myself. I want to know what it *says*, period, that's all, and I'll figure out what it means myself. Okay?"

"But you're just going to put your own religion in there, so what's the difference?"

"Well, I can try not to. And at least I won't consciously do it. And even if I inadvertently do it, I'll pick it up later and fix it."

"You'll want people to read your translation, right? That's pushing your stuff."

"No, it's just for me. My own studies. That's all."

"Then why," she asked suspiciously, "do you say grace every time you eat?"

"I don't, actually. I mean, I'm sure it looks like I do. Generally I do. But sometimes I don't at all. Or sometimes I try to have a thankful attitude. Or sometimes I forget or just don't care. Or I wait and thank him some other time. I mean, what's the difference?"

"Maybe it makes a difference to God."

"I can't believe that. I really just can't believe that, I'm sorry. Would you want a relationship like that with someone? You know, with doing mechanical things and not failing to do them? Wouldn't you rather be a little more relaxed. Wouldn't you rather have trust than scrutiny in a relationship?"

"I think you have to have both. I mean, realistically."

I sighed again. "I suppose."

"You can't get rid of religion."

"I'm not trying to eradicate it. I know it has to be there. There must be an expression of a truth, or at least the expression must be a given. There has to be some religion if there's faith. But for me, reducing the expression means a greater appreciation of the truth."

Then she said, "I know organized religion's a mess. The Catholic Church is run by men. I think women should be ordained. Why do we put up with this? It's stupid. Women do all the work, anyway. Men just wear the robes and take in the money."

"It's a pretty stupid world." I tipped up my bottle of water.

She shook her head. "I wouldn't say it's stupid. I mean, what the hell is that? That's cynical, and that doesn't help anybody. I say, when the world's stupid, fix it." She was quite animated, and when I didn't respond she continued, "The Catholic Church is like an army tank, heavy armor, in your face, its big threatening gun like a dick. Its whole attitude is very male, don't you think?"

"It's often accused of being the other way around."

"Well, I think its attitude is frigging male!"

I shrugged. "I don't know. I'm not Catholic."

"Well, I am, and I can tell you the Catholic Church is sexist."

Chuckling, I said, "And the Protestant sector of Christianity isn't sexist, right?"

"Your point?"

"Humanity can't be sexual and not have sexism somewhere." I shrugged. "People want the sexes to be different, but then complain of sexism. I mean, the whole glamour thing practically demands it. And Valentine's Day is a *what*, might I ask?"

Icily she said, "Sexism is wrong."

"Well, you just mean its wrong where it goes too far, and where it goes too far is where it crosses the line that *you've* drawn, right?"

"Well, I know it's wrong in church."

"Okay. But it's a given, it's going to be there, that's all. Just let it go. Work around it."

"So, you prescribe cynicism."

"No, I'm just trying to see both sides. I mean, fix it if you want to, who cares?"

"*I* care," she blurted.

"Okay, so, fix it."

"It should be changed, that's all. I would vote to have women in the priesthood. That's where I want them, and I would vote for it."

"Sure," I replied. "It just doesn't matter to me. Fine. Change it. I'll vote for it. You're just changing the configuration. Religion is like a big piece of living art. It doesn't matter what the configuration is, as long as it represents what the artist feels or thinks or whatever."

"I want women in the priesthood," she said with finality. "Maybe not back in the twentieth century, but at least now. Definitely now."

"Well, fine. It's your canvas. Paint it like you want. Put your own reality into it. Just do it. The artist should do what he wants."

"*She* wants," she corrected.

"Fine. I think the real value of religion is that it images faith. And I think most people see it that way. They don't care how you do your religion, just don't expect them to do the same."

"That's easy to say. But it's a powerful church."

"So, start a new church. Make it like you want."

"We will."

After a moment I asked, "How about women in combat?"

"War is male," she said. "Women help people. They're nurturers not destroyers."

"I would think you'd hate men, with all your negative encounters."

"You mean, a lesbian? No, I like men."

"How's it working out at the nursing home?"

"I have to get another TB test. The one I took somehow showed positive."

The ping pong game suddenly ended, and prompted perhaps by the cessation of its sounds for our background, we collected our things, deposited our cartons in a trash container, and left. Outside we stood at the corner, reluctant to part and return to work. The traffic noise made us raise our voices.

"Why did you want to become a nun?" I asked.

"That's a pretty big question to ask waiting for the light." But when I laughed she drew a deep breath. "I really don't know. I was just a girl. I think it all seemed magic, like a magnet, a force. I think I just had to bow down to something and felt that someday I'd submit to the church that way. I don't know if it was beautiful or ugly, scary or friendly. It was just magic or something. What was it for you?"

Imagining the blond hair hidden under a habit, I said, "Uh, I think it was kind of magic. Yeah, that term works. And solitude. I was looking for solitude."

"You have that now."

I looked at her. "Yes. I suppose I do." Then I looked up at the sky, which had turned darker.

"I think you have a rebel's heart," she ventured.

Imagining her hair as wet, I replied, "I suppose."

"Were you a hippie?"

"No," I said. "I felt the pull but rebelled against it."

She laughed and then asked, "Did you do drugs?"

"No. I drank a little, but I never took drugs. Did you want to be a hippie?"

"I wanted to, yes," she said, nodding. "I did want to."

"What stopped you?"

"I don't know. The definitions of life. What can I say? The way I grew up. All the stuff around me."

"I think you were a rebel yourself, though," I said.

"Oh, yeah. Maybe too much of one."

"Did you see *Dances With Wolves*?"

"Where the Indians were made out to be good and the soldiers bad? At least, *I* thought so."

"Yes," I said. "It did seem that way. But it didn't matter to me, because I was for the wolf."

She laughed. "I can see that. Yeah, I can see that."

Then, watching the clouds, I asked, "See you after work?"

"Sure." And then, in sync with a green light, she turned and crossed the street.

Chapter 4

The ambient noise on the express was usually too distracting to allow us to converse without shouting, so we sat in the din and let the few minutes pass. Occasionally I glanced at her hair, her skin, her dark glasses, turning my head far to the left to do so. As the train slowed at Fern Rock she said, "I'd invite you over, but I think I just need to crash."

Wearily I replied, "Yeah. Me too."

But then later, as the 70 bus approached my stop she turned from looking out the window and touched my arm. "No. Come over. Please. We'll watch something. Come for dinner."

About an hour later, after giving Raggie, Sono, and Tai Ping their evening meal and spending some time with them out in the yard, I gave them each a long hug and left for Brenda's. As I made my way along the broken sidewalk under the gracious trees my mind seemed to slow down and I thought of Helga. During her ten years with me following her adoption, she would wait each morning until I was dressed and had attached my keys to a belt loop before arising from her sleeping mat in the corner to follow me to the studio. There she would wait patiently while I took medicine and readied my shoulder bag for work. Then she would descend the back stairs with me, and later with Ragnar and Sono, to the kitchen, and finally the short steps, to be let out into the yard. Every morning now, I missed her and it seemed I always would. As I stepped carefully to navigate the uneven sidewalk, my thoughts went so strongly to her that I seemed to see her moving at a half run through a viridian field under a phthalocyanine sky. Her paws so lightly touched the ground that I anticipated her breaking into a run. She was so very beautiful, the field so intensely bluish-green, the sky so deeply blue. And then, as she drew a little nearer to me she suddenly turned her magnificent head and looked directly into my face, and somehow, as she did so and my eyes met hers, I knew she was happy. And I knew that she wanted me to know that there was nothing for her to forgive. Then, still at a half-run, as she passed close to me she faced forward and, as if to say there would be no more goodbyes, broke to full speed and ran, as it seemed, just for the joy of running. Watching her run, her massive tail stretched out in a silver streak, was like watching one of God's fastest angels flash across the heavens.

Pushing the button beside Brenda's name, I waited to hear footsteps on the inside stairs. Then through the thick glass I thought I saw her face below a blue scarf. The heavy door was swung open and I stepped closer.

Tilting her head, she said, "So, come on up."

"Hey, no sunglasses."

She closed the door and turned the lock. "Not tonight."

"And I haven't seen you in a scarf before. Kind of Dutch."

"I've been cooking. You don't want to find a hair in your food."

Following her up the uncarpeted stairs, I ventured, "I smell curry."

"My landlady's Indian. We're not having curry."

The aroma of cooking rice met me as I was ushered into the apartment's front room. I handed her the two bottles of spring water I was supposed to bring and glanced around. A large picture of the Virgin Mary hung between two windows and a smaller one, of a woman with a flag, rested on the mantle above a plastered-over fireplace. A crucifix hung above a side table.

In the direction of the Virgin I said. "The serene Lady."

"Yes."

And toward the mantle. "Joan of Arc?"

"Of course. Sit down. It'll be a few minutes."

Sinking into a soft recliner, I closed my eyes and surrendered to a seemingly irresistible desire to rest that had come upon me during the last few moments. It was always like that. No second wind. In what felt like seconds but must have been longer I heard her say that it was ready and I could come in. Incredibly weary, I struggled from the chair and forced myself to walk toward her voice.

"Your chair's comfortable," I said as I entered the kitchen. "I didn't want to get up."

"Well, my furniture isn't going to be as soft as yours."

"Why?"

"No dog hair," she teased.

"Good point. Hey, this is a neat kitchen. No dropped ceiling, huh? How did you stop them from that?"

"I didn't," she replied, filling a glass from one of the bottles. "I moved in this way. The landlady doesn't have a lot of money."

The simple setting of pork chops, stewed tomatoes over rice, and green beans seemed to add to the quaintness of the little kitchen. As I savored the coziness of the warm room, I asked, "Anything I can do?"

"No. Just sit," she said and as I did so, "I have blue glasses to match the plates."

"I like blue."

"Aren't you impressed?"

"Yep." I looked at the glass as she set it before me.

Pulling up her chair, she said, "So, grace?"

I hesitated. "Um, maybe that would be presumptuous in your house."

"Oh." And then she said, with a gentle edge to her voice, "Well, what about at lunch? Is giving thanks there honoring someone else's presence?"

"Well, I try to be discrete," I offered. "But here I think I should be, maybe, more discrete."

"Oh, please." Now she was teasing and the edge was gone. "Feel free. I don't care."

"No, no," I teased back. "It's your house."

Her eyes twinkled. "Like in *The Sand Pebbles*, where he said it was their rice bowl?"

"Something like that."

Reaching for the plate of pork chops, she said, "So, would you say a prayer to Mary if I wanted?"

"You're witty tonight." I took the plate.

"Just use your fork."

I did and then held the plate for her to take a piece. "I think you trapped me with a nice woman, a good meal."

"You can't see me blushing, can you?"

"No."

"That's because I'm not blushing."

Tasting a piece of pork chop with the rice and tomatoes, I said, "This is so good."

"Thank you."

"What's the seasoning?"

"Garlic powder."

"And the rice. I love rice and tomatoes."

"I'm glad. It's just simple. I'm glad you like it."

As we fell silent I imagined the movement of her pale eyes. It was remarkable, I thought, how the waiting area at Dr. Wu's, usually full at that

Saturday morning hour, had been empty, giving Helga a comfortable place to spread out on the tile floor before the examination. She did spread out, her great length reaching nearly to the opposite chairs. And then the examination revealed a large fast-growing tumor deep in her ear, very painful to the touch, soon to be unbearably painful, and virtually inoperable. Her intelligent sad eyes seemed aware that life's smile had come to an end. I would never forget saying then that I wanted to put her to sleep. The life expectancy for German Shepherds was about ten years. Helga was twelve. And I would not forget Dr. Wu's nod and the rapid preparation of the injection as the nurse trimmed a spot on Helga's foreleg. Then the quick administration of the injection. As I gently clasped Helga's long snout and looked into her eyes I saw no fear or agitation. I did not perceive that she was unhappy, but simply, somehow, ready. With her head in my hands, I felt her slump suddenly and slide into her sleep as the injected fluid took effect. I had bathed her the night before and she lay there all clean and fluffy as Dr. Wu listened through his stethoscope for the last beating of her heart. Then I heard him say she was gone. The waiting room had filled with patients and their keepers when I went out to pay the bill. I would never doubt that God had earlier provided that it should be clear of other dogs or cats that might disturb Helga. I would always believe that he had answered her life of faithful service by clearing the path for her to come to the other side in peace.

"You seem thoughtful," Brenda said.

"Oh," I replied. "Yes. I was just remembering someone." And with her inquisitive look I recalled walking into the house with the empty leash in my hand and having Raggie and Sono sniff the leash and look up at me as if to ask where Helga was.

"Do you think you live in the past? I learned in a class at night school that everybody has either a past, present or future perspective. What's yours?"

"Past," I answered, setting down my glass. "Pretty much past, I think. How about you?"

She shook her head. "I don't know. I do find myself recalling stuff I should just let go. When I was a kid I was asked to be part of a kind of honor guard, or whatever, to represent my school at a funeral for a neighborhood family. They had all died in a fire. Their row house had somehow caught fire during the night. I find myself dwelling on the image of their six caskets passing before us, one by one."

"So, which would you say?"

"I like to think I have a future perspective most of the time. It's a better way for me."

"Shake the baggage off?"

"Truly. As much as possible."

"So, you're a person of hope."

"Aren't you? I mean, even if you live in the past, you can have hope for the future. Aren't you a person of hope?"

I wished I could see more of her face. I didn't answer, but simply smiled toward the face below the blue scarf.

Chapter 5

A very bright sun was shining into the studio as I set my teacup beside the old paint box. The outside of the cup was intact, but the inside was filled with cracks. This was understandable, I thought, for while the outside had only to weather the atmosphere and the bumps and scrapes that came its way, the inside had to bear the boiling heat. But what did it matter, since the destiny of both facades was to perish with the whole? The dogs, two on the bare floor in the hall and one on a throw rug in the studio, lay in a glorious stupor, luxuriously digesting their breakfast. They were in heaven to have me with them, and I to be with them. I had taken my immunomodulator and was settling down for a tea-and-cookies moment to plan the day's work. I wouldn't know if my vision was good enough to allow me to paint, until I had worked for awhile under the long fluorescent light and two full-spectrum lamps. On some days, resting periodically from fatigue, I could paint from early in the morning well into the evening. But on others I had to stop after only an hour or two, clean up, and walk away from it, hoping for better vision on a better day.

Taking a bite of a fig bar and then a sip of the dark oolong tea, I slouched in my old chair to consider the drafts that hung from nails in the walls. The new Matisse book had been interesting but not helpful. Perhaps the little Chagall book, covering his early life in Russia, would send some piece of information down the corridor of inspiration. I knew Brenda would be starting her day with her usual coffee and donut. As I took another sip of tea and thought of emailing her that I was spending the day in the studio, an MS electric shock ran its course down my right side, from neck to foot.

Finishing the tea, I reached for a twenty by thirty draft of Black Moshannon. Tai Ping stirred as I stepped over him but then dropped his head back to the floor to watch me through enigmatic eyes. Placing the draft on the easel's shelf, I could see for the first time that its sky clashed with its bog water. Trying to outmaneuver the fluctuating color, acuity and fields in the deteriorating vision had become indescribably frustrating. Unconsciously I flexed my hands and rubbed my forearms to ascertain the progression of tingling. Overall the picture was promising, but while its composition survived my scrutiny, its form and color did not. The job of fixing it all looked to be very ugly and protracted.

Tai Ping lay quiet as I moved around the room, picking my way through other possibles. The abstracts looked good. The gallery had sold only one of the moon abstracts, but none of the scratchiest, linear, or spatial. Now all they wanted from me was landscapes, mostly the oil Black Moshannons. From a vertical stack of drafts I lifted a moon picture that was really a courtyard or houses-within-walls scene like *Fish Out Of Water* had ended up a few years before. Typically these pictures took a long time to evolve, since they were worked using multiple layers of heavily mediumed acrylic paint. But their end effect, that their objects had been enclosed in tinted plastic, was so wonderful as to make any effort worth it. Hoping I would not lose heart before it was finished, I returned it to the stack.

After finally selecting another acrylic draft, I filled both the spray bottle and brush cup with water from the bathroom sink, adjusted the side lamps, sat down, and pushed the CD remote's power button. Bruckner's second, already in the changer's fifth slot, soon opened. I loved painting to Bruckner. With a large palette knife I scooped gloss medium from its gallon bucket on the painting table at my left and plopped it into the center of the plastic palette at my right. After checking the proximity of Tai Ping's ear to the chair's castor, I rolled forward just enough to reach the tubes in the box of acrylics and then pushed the remote's volume plus button twice. As the cap to the phthalo blue was stuck from dried paint, I loosened it with the pliers. Acrylic was like that, drying so fast and tight that even on a second day of painting the caps to many of the tubes were stuck. The quinacridone red had further crystallized in its tube, so I had to break it down with more than the usual amount of medium. When a wave of sickness, not nausea but unwellness, passed over me, I wanted to go back to bed, but instead I grabbed the spray bottle, spread a mist above the palette, and waited for it to fall over the fresh paint. Then I took a number fourteen brush from a group on the table and set to work.

Just before noon I dropped my brush into the water cup and with Tai Ping as escort went down to the basement to wash the palette. Then I let out all three dogs into the backyard, dumped a can of beef vegetable soup into a saucepan, and poured a sizeable portion of salted sourdough pretzels onto a paper plate. When the soup boiled I let the dogs in, and we settled down to a relaxing lunch.

For the next hour, supplied with oolong tea and fig bars, I worked on the translation. Raggie and Ping wanted out, but Sono stayed to curl up on the couch beside my pile of books. From its protective pouch I extracted the dome-shaped magnifier I had recently ordered and pulled the old *Seventh Collegiate* close for another test run before setting to work on the translation. Fascinated with the power of the magnifier, I couldn't resist using it first as a toy nearly every time I needed it as a tool. Even before vision loss I had found the tiny type of normal book print, like that of the *Seventh Collegiate* dictionary, difficult to navigate, and having the seemingly microscopic print made accessible was as much fun as it was helpful.

After another session of painting, I washed the palette at five, took the day's second installment of meds, and cleaned up a little in the kitchen for Brenda to come at six for dinner. When the doorbell rang, the dogs, ecstatic over another opportunity to show they were serious guardians, roared through the house and slammed their paws against the inner front door.

"Hey," I said as I opened the outer front door. "I got your email."

"Yep." Handing me a loaf of Italian bread in a white paper bag, she stepped in wearing a white skirt and green short-sleeved top. It was a green that naturally made such things as blond hair stand out. A plain, flat silver cross was at her neck. Ritualistically removing the clip-on lenses, she said, "Whew, it's warm out there."

"Yeah. Pretty warm. Studio's hot."

"Maybe it's all those hot models."

"Could be."

"So, where's the imperial guard?"

"Right there."

"I was kidding," she said. "I saw them even from outside. You must have a lot of mail left out by the bushes."

"The mail carrier's kind of used to it, but solicitors do have a tendency to back away."

"Yeah," she said with a laugh. "The gospel's worth a lot, but not that."

A quiet meal prepared us for the tranquility of the evening. As dusk settled over our niche in the cosmic wall, the typical sounds of a summer evening began to whisper.

"I brought *A Walk In The Clouds*," she said. "Have you seen it?"

"No."

"For the populace," she said, smiling. "But nice. Very nice for tonight, I think." As she rose from inserting the disk into the player a light glinted from the silver cross.

As the film drew us into the story of its lovers and we sank deeper into the couch, the dogs left, one by one, to roam the house in search of cooler corners. I don't usually follow the plot of a film, which seems to be annoying to most people I watch a film with. When they laugh, I don't get it; and when I laugh, they usually turn and look at me. Since my focus is usually on aesthetic and technical aspects, I rarely know who the minor or even major characters are. With *A Walk In The Clouds,* however, it was different, and for some reason I was immediately engaged by the plot. During a scene where the lead characters waved fans to blow heated air across their vineyard to save the endangered fruit from frost, I observed, "She's really perspiring."

"Yes."

"He seems a little warm, too."

"Yes."

When I felt Ragnar's nose nudge my hand I pushed the pause button and got up to let the dogs out. When I returned I switched on a light and saw Brenda's outstretched hand.

"Help me up," she said. "It's good to take a break. So, what does *Tai Ping* mean?"

"Great Peace."

"Does he make it more secure for you here?"

"I hope so. I think so. You know, your hair shines even in the dark."

"You just turned the light on."

"I know, but I saw it before."

"You could see that?"

"Yeah. Easily. The glow from the screen."

"By the time I was eleven my hair was all white."

"The Lithuanian side?"

"Who knows?"

In the kitchen I put ice in glasses. "Something clear or cola?"

"Clear."

"Was your hair long when you rode the motorcycle?"

"Yeah, it was long. And no helmets in those days. Why?"

I wrinkled my nose. "I don't know. What was he like?"

"I told you," she said, impatience in her voice. But then, "He had been a paratrooper. He had the most perfect body I've ever seen on a man. He was odd too, though. I mean, he wasn't idyllic or anything like that. He was wonderful, but not idyllic. Small toes. He was quite strong. He was artistic too. He made things. If he'd been an artist he would have done nudes of me."

"Then you could have had your out-of-body experience in the nude."

"That might've worked." An odd expression on her face, she backed against the kitchen sink, as if for support. "He was gone that day, the whole day. I was bored out of my mind. It was a good thing I didn't believe in suicide. I read. I walked around the apartment. I watched his stupid broken television. Everything was stupid and wretched. Then, about the middle of the afternoon, I just flopped back on his bed and stared at the ceiling. Maybe I went to sleep or something, I don't know, but I don't think it was a dream. I never thought it was a dream. All I know is that I was floating above me, looking down at myself on the bed. And then I was looking up at the ceiling again, and I sat up. I was, like, really, really scared. It was so, so weird."

"Did it ever happen again?"

"No. Just that once."

"So, he really liked you?"

The odd expression again. "I don't know. I think he did. He certainly seemed to like my body. But he was a drinker, like I told you. He had problems from the war. He'd be fine for awhile, okay with everything—himself, me, the world. He didn't talk much about things. He just didn't talk much. When he did he was articulate, he was fine. He was just generally locked up. If he had talked it out, he may have been okay and not needed to drink himself stupid."

"Is that why you talk to me?"

"Maybe," she said. " Maybe."

"So, what happened?"

"You want to hear it again?"

"Sure."

She rolled her eyes. "I was still just a kid. I started going out with my friends, just for a good time. I needed friends my own age. He didn't have friends at all. People he drank with, but no friends, nobody he trusted. He let me go out with my friends. But then he started getting scared, maybe. It was like he was paranoid or something. But he could see it. He could see we were starting to break up. He knew it was going to happen. Maybe it was the inevitability of it that bothered him. Then, well, we broke up. He wrote me strange letters after that. He went a little nuts, I think." She sighed. "Are you psychic at all?"

I had been looking at her hair. "I don't know," I answered. "Maybe a little. I've been told I am."

"Did you ever have an out-of-body experience?"

"No," I replied, looking toward the window. "It's cooler now. I always seem to breathe better when it turns cooler."

"Yes, it's cooler. It's nice. It's been a nice evening."

Chapter 6

On a day in late October a quiet rain fell scattered and benign across the city, intensifying the beauty of the season's dying leaves. My wool sport jacket gave me the conscious feeling that I was comfortable and secure despite the chilly autumn dampness. During the subway ride I tapped out on the PDA the beginning of a new diary entry.

In my office the desktop's low-vision configuration, which I had set to produce white characters on a black background, was soon giving me what seemed like pink characters on a purple-brown background, so I looked away for a moment to rest my eyes. But the walls and ceiling seemed to glow in dirty-yellow. I concluded, however, that I was not having an attack. I closed my eyes and thought of Helga, who would say no more goodbyes. Her eyes had said there was nothing to forgive. She had attempted to free me from my guilt over having put her to sleep. Her attempt had failed. Whether she felt there was something to forgive or not, I knew, somehow, deep in my mind, that I would always be guilty.

Peering through the hanging magnifier, I opened my email and checked for incoming messages. Then I clicked on Compose, Address Book, Personal, and finally bcollins to fill in the top of the Compose box. After a moment I typed, *Good morning, Brenda—I don't think Braille is for me.*

How are things going today? Waiting for the reply, I checked the other messages for work requests from the faculty.

Then, there she was. I clicked and read, *What are you doing this evening?*

It was a little after six when we took a booth at the restaurant, broke apart chopsticks, and began to sample the bowls of spiced vegetables. Korean words and phone numbers covered our paper place mats. I knew the woman who served us, or at least had occasionally seen her working there for about a year. Apparently she spoke only a few words of English. She was not glamorous, but like most people, was beautiful in her own way. Whenever I would request after a meal a container to take the remnants home to the dogs, she insisted on filling the container for me, and I watched in silence until she had placed all in the paper bag. Once, after I had ordered a cola and ice, she said with a kind of humble conviction, pointing to the soda, "Tea better." They were the only English words I had ever heard her speak.

"Did you get your dogs fed?" Brenda asked as she closed her chopsticks on a piece of spiced cucumber.

"Yep. I don't like running in and out like that, but this is nice. It was a good idea."

"Troubled?"

"Not really. I wish I could have spent more time with them. They wait for me all day. Then when I have to go out, it bothers them."

"Bothers them?"

"It was the look they gave me, that's all."

"Look?"

"It's not important. It's okay. Really, this is very nice. You make it nice. It was a good idea. Thanks."

"But the dogs win, right?"

I sighed. "Not really. I just don't want to hurt their feelings. They can't talk. They just look at me. They're all rescue dogs. They were abandoned or just dropped off at the shelter. I remember how they looked in their cages there. And then I adopted them, one by one. But when I brought them home they all gave me the same look that said don't ever leave me."

"I know," she said. "it's okay. There are people I think about. I don't want to hurt them either."

Looking down at the place mat, I said, "Korean words are neat. Like in a block."

Then for a short while we did not speak. We did not look at each other but at other people and toward various places around the room. And we listened to the low general chatter, as if we should not be talking but listening.

Finally, she said, "This morning I heard a rattling in the backyard and found a squirrel caught in a trap. The neighbor had put it on his trash can."

"A humane trap?"

She nodded. "Know what I did? I went over and opened it and let him go. Boy, did he run. It was like he flew from the trap the moment I opened it. I thought he might bite me."

"Why did you do it?"

She was thoughtful. "I don't know." With her eyes following an elderly couple who seated themselves in the adjacent booth, she said, "I like it here. I hate the long onion things they serve with the beef." She glanced around the room, which was starting to fill with patrons. "How was work?" she asked.

"Okay. I think someone might try to get into my office."

"What? Why?"

"I work on exam material."

"You lock your door at night, don't you?"

"Yeah. Even when I go to the bathroom or to get water from the fountain for my tea boiler."

She stared at me. "What are you going to do?"

"Nothing. Just make sure I never forget to lock the door."

"You think a lot about security, don't you?"

"I guess."

"You can only be so safe. And then, just take your chances."

"I guess. You know, the food here can be really hot."

"I've only been here once. You shouldn't eat too much spice before the meal comes."

"You're right," I said, putting down the chopsticks.

"Do you think I'm being a mother?"

"Not really. Maybe just an Aquarian. You're right, I shouldn't. It's bad for the reflux."

"My sister thinks I'm always being a mother. I ask her things like anybody else would. How often she goes over to Mom's and stuff like that. But that's not like asking her how many times a week she and her husband have sex."

Since she was waiting for a response, I said, "No, you're right."

Leaning forward, she asked, "Let me ask you. Do you like kissing women?"

I hesitated. "Do you like kissing men?"

"Yes. Who did you date in high school?"

I gave a short laugh. "That's a long time ago. I *have* dated since, you know."

"But who did you date in high school?"

"Well, the girl I dated the longest had brown hair with bangs and was a little taller than I was. Her parents were kind of rich, or at least I thought they were. We didn't have a lot. We weren't really poor, but we didn't have a lot. The difference between her family and mine made me feel poor. Her father owned a furniture store. She was cute. Very thin. I really liked her a lot. I think I loved her. But she would buy me things my parents couldn't afford, like an expensive shirt for my birthday. It was things like that. We went together for about a year, and then one day I just broke up with her."

"She was rich and *you* broke up with *her*. Why?"

"I knew it wouldn't work. The relationship was doomed, that's all. It was, like, a constant collision of rich and poor. And she was always reminding me of the disparity, or at least I thought she was. Maybe I was self-conscious about it. I know I always felt guilty about not having money."

"Why didn't you get a job?"

"Actually, I think that's the key to the whole thing. I could have, but I just didn't want to. And I knew I didn't want to. Worse, I knew I *wouldn't* want to. I sensed there was something in me that didn't care about money. It wasn't that I saw money as bad. I just couldn't force myself to care."

"What did you care about?"

"I didn't actually know." I gave another short laugh. "The truth is, I was confused. I remember an English teacher in high school taking me aside. I had failed some test, and she was really angry. She said my testing showed that I should be whizzing school. She said I shouldn't be getting a perfect score on one test and then failing the next, when it was basically the same material. She said the testing showed I should be understanding anything I wanted to." I shook my head.

"What?"

"You know, I couldn't even find my way around the school building. I was confused human being. Everybody else seemed to know everything. I didn't seem to know anything. The teacher wanted me to care about the class and grades and knowing the material. I mean, give me a break. I was too confused to know what to care about."

"What did the girl say when you broke up with her?"

"She was furious. She said something like she would've been willing to live in a shack with me if necessary." Again I shook my head. "Poor girl. Totally deceived. I would simply have been forced to go to college and then move out into the work force. I mean, I would have done it myself. It was the dynamic of the whole thing."

"What would have been wrong with that? You're in the work force now."

"I know, but in my own time and on my own terms. No. I would have self-destructed."

After a moment she asked, "What color were her eyes?"

"I don't remember. Brown, I think. Yeah, maybe brown. You know, it's funny, but years later, in a fit of sentimentality, I sent her a birthday card and wrote, 'To the girl I will never forget to remember,' which was quite stupid. The whole relationship was my fault."

"How could it have been your fault if you were so confused?"

I looked at her. "I don't know."

"You really are guilt-driven, aren't you?"

"Seems that way."

"You should've been a Catholic."

Then she was silent, and I knew she was thinking about the information she had gathered. I reflected that Lithuania bordered both Poland and Russia. Although she had seemed willing to be open about some parts of her past, she had been quite secretive about the rest. It was odd how she always kept her purse within reach. I considered that if she had a gun it was not bigger than a three-eighty. Her wrists were too slight to handle nine-millimeter recoil in a frame small enough to fit in that purse. I knew the Russians were sending people over to live in the United States, to permeate the society, to meld, to become Americans. And it was not only the Russians who were doing this. There were others.

Suddenly she asked, "Who else?"

"What?"

"Who else did you date in high school?"

"Uh, well, there was the artist. Red hair—well, reddish. Beautiful girl. Possibly Irish, but I never asked."

"So, did you sleep with these girls?"

I looked at her for a moment. "Does it matter?"

"No."

When iron pots of hot rice were set on the table and the rest of the meal arrived I said, "I'm hungry and I'm not hungry."

"Yes."

And then I said, "No, I didn't sleep with them."

Glancing at my face and then away, she said, "It doesn't really matter. This chicken looks good."

"Yes, it does. Things do matter, though, don't you think?"

"Of course. Why else would you say grace, or do your translation, or paint?"

"But I mean not just to me or you, but per se, right?"

"Of course."

"You're certain?"

"Yes, I am," she said, obviously irritated.

I looked at her hair and then down at her face again. "So, it matters that we're sitting here together."

"Yes," she said. "It does matter."

Later in the evening I peered through a kitchen window into an unusually dark backyard. I would not be able to get the ladder out until daylight to replace the floodlight's bulb. Backing away suddenly as my nose touched the cold pane, I strained to catch the moonlight on the dogs as they sniffed and prowled. But I could see nothing. I thought of how Brenda's hair had been so beautiful in the soft lighting of the restaurant and how later, as we stood in front of her apartment, I had tried to imagine that I could still see it under the October moon. I pulled a chair from the table and sat to wait for the dogs to scratch at the door to be let in. Even though the fence's wire gate had once been unlatched from the outside by someone in the night, I knew the dogs would secure the yard before coming in. I removed the clothespin from a bag of pretzels and then replaced it, deciding to wait for the dogs, who loved helping me with late-night snacks. But Helga would not be coming in with them. Lowering my head to my arms on the table, I thought of the dream and how from the depths of the ocean the wave had arisen to claim me. How it had come in, lifted itself to a great height, crossed the beach, and fallen upon me. How I had known in my own depths that God had sent it. And how, afterward, I was not able to think of the dream as a nightmare, as its wave had come from God. I raised my head and lowered it again. Not only the kitchen but the universe, it seemed, was unbearably ugly. Soon the dogs would scratch at the door and I would let them in and we would all be safe.

Sometime after eleven I switched off the light and got into bed. I pulled the covers up over my ear and felt under the pillow to make sure the chambered Tokarev was on half-cock. Turning my head, I listened. But I could hear no sound of anyone outside. Ragnar was curled up in her sheepskin bed in the bathroom and Sono was snuggled on the studio couch in the middle bedroom. Tai Ping was just beginning to find a suitable place on the bed to sleep beside me. The corner where Helga had slept was empty. In perhaps the last moments before I slept I thought of Brenda as we had said good night at her front door. In the moonlight I had not been able to see her face very clearly. But it must have been beautiful, for it was beautiful now even as it lost reality behind my closed eyes.

JUDY

Chapter 1

I first saw her as she sat at her desk at the elementary school in Jacksonville. Although she seemed to be alone, somehow I felt I should keep my voice low.

"Ms. Morino?"

She looked up and responded enthusiastically, "Yes. Mr. Le Haley? Come in. Hi."

"Hi," I replied and then took the center aisle to her desk, where I shook her hand.

Her hair, which just touched her shoulders, seemed to be graying brown and was blazed with a shock of white. All of it, I presumed, had been kept natural. She seemed to be nearly my height as she turned a plastic chair toward me and then repositioned herself behind the desk. I folded the cane as I sat, and continued to hold it as discretely as possible.

"I am so glad you could come, Mr. Le Haley. I just love your work. I've been looking forward to this so much, I just can't tell you. My kids are *so* excited."

"Thanks," I replied, absorbing her genuine smile, and then added awkwardly, "I'm Stanly."

"Well, I'm Judy. That's fine."

"I'm sorry to come early, like this."

"That's okay, really. I'm glad to see you. I thought you might have gotten in, but wasn't sure. I was going to give you a call this evening."

Glancing around, I said, "You have a very attractive classroom." But immediately I knew I had lied. It was not the classroom, it was the woman.

"Thanks," she replied. "I'm glad you like it." She looked at me for just a moment and then said, "You know, I was so excited when I got your email that you could come down and give a talk to my class and spend the week with us. It's great. The kids are going to love it."

After judging her demeanor to be about half private and half public, I responded, "Yes, well, I'm looking forward to it. Good. I know I wasn't scheduled to come to your class until tomorrow, but I thought I'd just kind of give it a peek and maybe take a look around at the school, see what has changed. Memories!"

My vision comfortably crossed the four or five feet to take in the thin shoulders and neck, the silver pendant, and the fashionable blouse. But then I wondered why my mind had made it silver instead of gold, as I really couldn't tell; and why I thought *fashionable,* when actually I couldn't have made such a discernment to save my life. And I was certain she had an air of upper middle class; but then, what was that and how would I know it? And an earthiness too, which intrigued me. But then, how would I know there was an earthiness, or anything else, about her? Why would my mind make up such pleasant things? But it wouldn't stop, and I guessed she was in her fifties.

"Oh, yes, that's fine, sure," she said. "I'm glad you came. We're on half-day today, so you can meet the class tomorrow. They were here until about eleven. It's a teacher's planning afternoon for us. Ugh. Actually I'm just grading papers. I hate taking them home. So, are you settled in?"

"Yes," I said enthusiastically. "Thanks for setting it up. The apartment seems quiet and I have the privacy I need. You know, could I ask where you're from. You don't have a Southern accent at all."

"Oh, no," she chuckled. "I'm from Philadelphia, too, or at least I taught near there, in a suburb. I'm a Jersey girl. I grew up in Mt. Holly."

"I can't believe this. Philadelphia. Wow. Okay."

"Well, I suppose that's life on a small planet, right?"

"Yeah," I said. "Tiny world."

"And in your emails you said you spent a lot of your childhood here in Jacksonville?"

"Yeah. Then we moved to New Jersey and I ended up in Philadelphia. But here I lived down on Harris Street, which is no longer there, I understand."

"Actually, I expected *you* to have a Southern accent, but you don't seem to have any distinct accent."

"A blend of a lot of things."

"Do you miss the South?"

"I think I do, really. Yeah, in many ways."

"Why?"

"I don't know," I said, looking from her hair to the blackboard behind her. "Nostalgia, I think. Memories are very powerful for me. Does the Jersey girl miss Jersey?"

She hesitated. "Yes, actually, I do."

"Why?" I asked, watching her earrings move.

She laughed. "I miss the Jersey tomatoes. Isn't that amazing? Tomatoes."

"They're good tomatoes, what can I say? You can grow them here, though."

"I do. But they're just not the same."

"You'll just have to come back to New Jersey."

"That would be nice," she said. "I'm getting to like Jacksonville. The hurricanes scare me, but it's really nice down here. The palm trees, the Spanish moss, mild winters. It's slower down here, more relaxed. But, yeah. I'll probably go back someday."

Hoping not to be rude, I checked my watch. "Well, listen, I guess I should go. Again, I hope I haven't bothered you. It was really good to meet you."

"No, no, that's fine. Yeah, I'm glad you came in. It was good to meet you, too."

I stood, the folded cane in my left hand, and said, "So, I suppose I'll see everybody tomorrow."

Rising, she extended her hand, "Yes, if you'll come about ten, I'll introduce you to the class and you can give your first talk."

"Sure. That'll be great. See you all then."

"*Y'all*," she corrected.

I laughed. "Oh, yes. Y'all."

As I turned she asked, "You'll be okay getting back?"

"Sure, just fine. Herschel Street seemed pretty familiar. My best friend used to live two blocks down. I'll be fine, thanks." Passing through the open doorway I turned to wave and noted that she had already raised her hand to wave back.

Then she asked, "You don't need your cane all the time?"

"No. Not really," I replied. And giving her an abbreviated wave, I walked down the hall.

Instead of returning to the apartment I took King Street at Herschel and walked toward the river until I passed St. Johns Avenue. Then, venturing as to where the miniscule Harris Street had run and our slanting wood-frame house had stood, I continued another hundred feet or so and faced where a small one-story brick house had stood beside a dirt alley. The whole corner of the block was covered with new structures that seemed to be part of the St. Vincent's Medical Center. Yes, the brick house was gone. The open porch was gone. The pigeon was gone. I stood for a moment, staring at where I judged the corner of the porch had been. And then I saw it all happen again. The feathers tufted out as one of the clustered chromed pellets from my hunting slingshot struck home. The pigeon's eye registered a terrible bewilderment as he paced frantically in the corner of the porch. Then apparently connecting the pain from the pellets with my actions he tried desperately to discover a way around me. But even at eleven my slight body was enough to block his escape. I quickly reloaded and shot again, but all three pellets of the cluster missed. As I again reloaded the slingshot's pouch I wondered why the pigeon did not simply fly up and out of the open sections above the porch's half walls. I thought that perhaps the first shot had really hurt him or that he had been caught by a cat and couldn't fly anymore. Sensing his entrapment, I pulled the slingshot's powerful surgical-tubing bands all the way back, aimed, and released the pouch. Again the pellets missed, but one, ricocheting somehow from the bricks, returned instantly and stung my cheek. Then as the creature's pacing grew more frantic I suddenly became ashamed and left the porch.

Turning away, I walked back to the apartment. With the cane propped in a corner, I sat in the rocker and imagined what the dogs were doing. Ragnar might be sleeping on the rusty mat outside the back door. Sono might be lying along the bricks of the patio. Tai Ping might be prowling by the back fence.

Chapter 2

Just before ten the next morning, I entered the classroom and closed the door as inconspicuously as I could. The entire class, who had apparently been working quietly, turned and stared. I smiled and gave a little wave to those near me. One girl, with glasses, waved back.

Judy was beside me in a moment and took my arm. "Are you all right?" she asked in a whisper.

"Yes, fine, thanks," I replied, also in a whisper. "I'll be okay. You go ahead. I'll follow."

As we walked between the desks to the front of the room the students turned, as if at a wedding. They were quiet until their teacher spoke.

"Class, I'd like you to meet Mr. Le Haley. He is an artist who lives in Philadelphia and has come to visit with us and talk to us about his art. He'll be with us for about an hour each for the rest of the week. Today, he's going to tell us a little about himself and then tell us about his art. Then we'll have a question-and-answer time. Tomorrow, we'll see a slide show of Mr. Le Haley's paintings. Remember, this is a note-taking exercise. For the rest of the week you will take notes on your note pads, and over the weekend you will rewrite them as a two-page report on Mr. Le Haley's visit. This is the sixth grade, and next year, in junior high, you will need to take notes throughout the day. This will be the last project this year for working on these skills. So, now, please welcome Mr. Le Haley to our class."

Recoiling from the enthusiastic applause that followed, I simply stood there and stupidly looked from blurry face to blurry face. Suddenly aware that my grip upon the cane, which I held before me like a stage prop, was inordinately tight, I relaxed and took a breath, my head dipping nervously. As the clapping waned and was superseded by a low rustling of paper Judy took her place on a folding chair as part of my audience.

"Well, hi, everybody," I said. "Ms. Morino has invited me to talk to you about art and low vision. When I started painting, almost forty years ago, my vision was fine. Then about six years ago I became ill with MS, multiple sclerosis, and that has left me almost blind. But fortunately I am still able to see just enough to keep doing art."

I had composed a simple talk in line with Judy's request to keep the focus on art rather than low vision. Following the introduction I spoke for about fifteen minutes on my daily routine in the studio and the steps needed for building a canvas and doing a painting. Then, steeling myself for the challenge of recognizing raised hands, I closed and asked for questions.

A boy on the front row, who for most of my talk had supported his head with his hands, half-heartedly raised his left hand and asked, "Why do you have a cane?"

"Actually, I didn't use a cane for a long time, because I thought it would be, you know, too much trouble. And I did pretty well. I mean, I didn't fall or anything. I had kind of a system for getting around in places where I couldn't see so well. But then one day I had a bad fall and knew that the vision was getting worse and that I needed to start feeling where to walk. So, I use a cane mostly for safety. I don't use it all the time. Like, at home I know my way around, but here at your school I don't. When I become completely blind I'll need to use it a lot more."

A girl behind him asked, "Do you have a dog?"

"I have three dogs. But, do you mean a guide dog?"

"Yes," she answered almost imperceptibly.

I shook my head. "No, I don't have a guide dog. They're really neat, though. A lot of blind people have them. I'm not sure I could take care of one, that's the problem. Every time we'd go out my other dogs would want to come along, and it would be a big disappointment for them to have to stay home. Do you know someone with a guide dog?"

Again the whisper, "Yes. Near my house. I petted him."

"Well, dogs who lead the blind are some of the world's greatest dogs. They are very well trained. First they're trained on their own, just to become a guide dog, and then they're trained with the blind or low-vision person they're going to help. They have helped blind people in so many ways. They help blind people to get around safely and are warm, happy companions for them, too. They usually wear a harness with a handle that sticks up for the blind person to hold on to. Guide dogs are trained to lead around obstacles, like chairs in a room or parking meters on a sidewalk. They help blind people to cross streets safely, which is very difficult at a busy intersection. There are many accounts where guide dogs have acted heroically to save the person they're leading. Then, after serving a person for a few years, a guide dog retires from service and is adopted by someone who wants to love them and give them a good home. As you can imagine, the waiting list for adopting a retired guide dog is very long."

Then a girl beside her asked, "Didn't you use to go to this school?"

"Well, yes, I did. A long time ago. I came here from the second through the sixth grade."

"Did you like it?"

"Yes, I did. I have very good memories of coming to this school. My name was Greg then. It was a nickname my parents gave me and I used it all the time until I went to junior high."

Then Judy said, "Yes, Jordan."

A boy that seemed to be near the middle of the class, whose raised hand I had missed, asked in a low voice, "Why do blind people wear sunglasses? Doesn't that make it worse?"

"No. If you're blind you can't see anything, so nothing makes it worse. But the answer is not really easy here, because some low-vision people have to wear dark glasses for a number of reasons. One reason is to protect the rest of their vision from damaging ultraviolet rays from sunlight. Another reason is sometimes that they can't tolerate regular bright light. With me, for instance, if light from even a tiny light bulb comes into my eye from a certain angle, it makes it almost impossible for me to see anything straight on. But nobody knows for certain why completely blind people have sometimes, at least in the past, chosen to wear dark glasses. The best answer I've heard suggested is that some blind people might wear them because they don't want to be stared at, even if they can't see the person staring at them. Does that make sense?"

"Why do people stare?"

"Well," I said, "sometimes blind people's eyes, because they can't see something to look at, kind of look to the side a little bit, and that looks maybe a little strange to sighted people. I think, though, that I myself would stare at a blind person's eyes because I would wonder what that person was thinking. You know, there in the darkness." In the silence that followed this I began to sense that Judy had risen from her chair. Then I heard her voice beside me.

"So, class, I think that's enough questions for today. Mr. Le Haley is tired and needs to rest," and turning to me, she added, "don't you, Mr. Le Haley?"

"Uh, well, yes. Yes, that'd be good."

"So, that's fine then," Judy said delightedly, nearly clapping her hands. But at the desk directly in front of us the girl raised her hand timidly, and Judy, with a reluctant nod, acknowledged her, "Yes, Terri?"

The hand dropped and the girl asked, "Mr. Le Haley, how much do paints cost?"

I swallowed. I could tell from the way she pushed her glasses back to the bridge of her nose that they were heavy. Judy's vivid description of her now seemed poignantly accurate. From a poor Irish family, she was quiet, intelligent, and yet genuine, with red-brown hair, sad eyes, and no sign of joy. I could not see the sad eyes, and for some reason I could not imagine them, but my mind had little difficulty putting melancholy upon the face. For an intelligent girl, she seemed strikingly uncommunicative. During my talk I had avoided looking at her, but as I peered now into the melancholy face I felt myself almost unable to look away. Swallowing again, I said, "Uh, you know, I . . ." Inexplicably, I could not continue. I thought of Helga, and then of Thor. My words had sent them both away. They had lived and served, and my words had sent them both away. Words were like that. They could do things like that. They could kill and they could make alive. At that moment I wished that fate had not placed me so close to the girl's desk. And then, for just an instant, I saw her eyes behind the thick lenses. Or perhaps I wasn't seeing them. Perhaps my brain had taken her voice or some combination of other data, made a best match from my memory of sad eyes, and then supplied an erroneous image.

Clumsily I said, "Well, they can cost a lot if you get them at an expensive store. But there are really neat mail-order places that have pretty reasonable prices. I usually shop online and try to get free shipping." But then I blinked slowly, realizing that she probably would never be able to order enough to qualify for free shipping. When she pushed her glasses up again and continued to look into my face, I said, in an attempt to be cheerful, "You know, I have tons of catalogs you could look at. I could send them to Judy and she could bring them to class." In the palpable hush that followed I felt the *eyes of a teacher upon me* and corrected myself. "I mean, *Ms. Morino.*"

And then Judy said firmly, "Class, we should let Mr. Le Haley go now, and tomorrow, he can come back and show slides of his paintings. Thank you, Mr. Le Haley." And with this she started the applause.

Turning from Terri's unassuming gaze, I said to the class, "Yes, thanks. Okay. Well, goodbye," Then, after giving an awkward wave, I walked to the back of the room, still holding the cane in front of me more as a prop than a tool, and opened the door and left.

It was late in the afternoon when Judy tapped at the apartment's door, a small wicker basket on her arm. Flipping the latch button, I opened the door and stood aside. "Hey," I said cheerfully yet suspiciously. "This is a surprise."

"Hello, mister gloomy," she said, handing me the basket. "I thought I'd come by and cheer you up."

After a moment I said, "Not so great, huh?"

"No, actually, you gave a nice talk."

"Gloomy?"

"Oh boy," she replied. She moved a worn manila folder of my translation papers and sat in its place. "*Gloomy* is a good term here, I think." Nodding, she added, "And we might think about *weird*."

I looked down. "I didn't mean to be."

"I've just driven a little girl home. She was in tears."

"I'm sorry. I didn't want to seem negative. . . . Not the Irish girl, I hope?"

"No," she sighed, "another girl. She's okay, though." She shook her head. "Don't worry about it."

"Don't worry about it? First I'm weird and now I'm not to worry about it?"

"Look, it's not important. I'm just over reacting."

"I didn't want to seem melancholy."

"Do you enjoy being blind, or something?"

"No."

"Why did you say *there in the darkness*? I mean, what is that? These are children."

I felt odd standing, perhaps since she was a teacher, so I sat on a folding chair across from her, holding the basket in front of me by its handle. "I've probably learned to be a little happy about it," I said. "The blindness world is kind of interesting."

After a moment she said, "Uh, look. Forget what I said. Tomorrow, just try to be happier, okay? Tell a joke or two. . . . Do you tell jokes?"

"Not very well. I don't get jokes very well myself. I do know a superman joke, but somebody dies in it."

"Uh, well, then, don't tell it. It's okay. Forget it."

"I could learn one. Do you know a joke I could tell?"

She stared at me and then said, "Just show the paintings and talk about them, okay? Try to think sunshine and happiness. Be cheerful."

"Okay, sure. I'll try. So, what's wrong with Terri's vision?"

The question seemed to be a relief and she relaxed and crossed her legs. She shook her head. "Well, it's not like with you. There's no condition. At least none they've told me about. She just has really poor vision. Legally blind, like I told you. What I want is for her to believe that she is free to create. She wants to be an artist. I know she does, I can see it in her. I want her to believe that her poor vision, even blindness if it comes, can't have any actual effect on her creativity. I want her to know that low vision is just an obstacle, something to work around. It might be aggravating for her and slow her down, but it can't stop her. Only her own heart can do that, and I wanted her to know it. She's a sad girl." She nodded and added, "I think you could encourage her, actually. You already have. What do you think?"

I raised my shoulders and answered, "I don't know." Nor, just then, did I want to know. For some reason, I only wanted to think about the woman in front of me at that moment, to look at her and to think about her. And so I did. Why did I find her to be so beautiful? Indeed, she was beautiful. No one would doubt that. But why did I find her beauty to be so magical? Nothing in me could give a reason, and yet nothing in me could doubt the reality of that magic. Looking at her hair, I tried to follow the edge of its natural wave down to her shoulder. It was wonderful, I thought, not to think about the students or their needs or the presentation or the paintings or anything else that smacked of responsibility, but just to sit across from this beautiful woman and appreciate the loveliness of her form. Earlier, in the classroom, the green-and-white stripped top, black pants and tan sandals seemed indistinct, as if part of some faded wallpaper. But now, with responsibility cleared from my mind, they seemed brilliant.

"Listen," she said, "the basket is for your dinner, if you want it. It's fried chicken. I thought it might help with your dinner."

"Help?"

"You know, because you can't get around so easily."

"I get around just fine," I said, trying not to sound ungrateful. "Thanks, though. That was really good of you. Thanks."

"Or if you don't want it now, you could put it in the refrigerator and I'll take you somewhere." Then quickly she stood, pulled the basket from my hand, opened its top, and extracted the box. "Here, let's put it in and go somewhere. I'll just take you. Come on, are you ready?"

I shrugged. "Uh, okay. I have to take some meds. I'm sorry. It'll only take a second. And I have to close the windows."

"I'll get the windows," she offered, mimicking me with a shrug of her own. "You go ahead."

In the bathroom I took out two immunomodulator tablets, two extra-strengths, and an acid blocker. Swallowing each of the pills with water, I listened as she moved about in the kitchen. The sounds of her closing a cabinet door and then each of the apartment's windows were eerie.

Half and hour later, at a pizzeria in Avondale, we sat in a window booth, sampled iced sodas, and waited for our order. With the late-afternoon sunlight showing its slide upon the table top between us, I watched the movement of her hands and imagining an occasional glitter from her jewelry. I stirred the ice in my soda and looked at the white section of her hair. The sounds of her closing down the apartment no longer seemed eerie, but comforting, and I wondered whether it would sound like that when people were closing me in for the last time. But then, I wanted to be cremated, as Helga had been.

"So, do you think this goes?" she asked, holding out her left arm.

I squinted at the various metal rings encircling her wrist. "It's quite a bracelet," I replied. "You mean, with the top or the pants?"

"Both."

"Yes. I think, maybe, it goes with both."

She sighed. "Well, do the pieces of the bracelet go with each other? There's silver and gold, sculpted and smooth. Does it all work or not?"

"I can't usually tell gold from silver, so maybe I'm not the one to ask."

"It doesn't matter. I want to know what you think. Do you think it works?"

"Uh, sure. Yeah. I think it does. And I think it goes with your hair too."

"Thank you."

Watching her draw soda through her straw, I asked, "Do you live in Avondale?"

"Yes. I bought a house here right after I came. A small single. But I have a nice yard and a garden."

"Which do you work in the most, the yard or the garden?"

"Oh, I just like to be out. It doesn't matter. I landscape the yard and change the flowers, and I grow tomatoes and vegetables in the garden. It's the sun I love, really, the wonderful sun."

"A lot of sun, huh?"

"Yes, of course. Tons of it. I have to have the sun. Are you a sun person?"

"Not really, no. Sorry."

"What are you, then?" she asked, with some distaste.

"Um, well, I'm kind of a rain person. I like the sun too. I like a variety. But yes, predominantly, rain, I think." I followed the contour of her face from cheekbone to chin and back up. "You could probably live in the islands, then, right?"

"Oh, yes. Ah, I would love to live there. Just after college I worked for a month with missionaries in the Dominican Republic. It was wonderful. So much sun. A quick rain, and then the sun again. I couldn't get enough of it. And the glorious beaches. I used to sneak away and just walk the beach."

Imagining her in a swimsuit, then a bikini. "My guess is, you couldn't live in Belgium, then. Rains three days out of five."

"Ugh. Depressing."

"I don't know. For me the rain is healing. Like the sun for you, right?" She seemed to be looking at my beard, and my hand went up automatically to make sure nothing was sticking out. I was glad I had trimmed it before leaving Philadelphia. Then I asked, "Are your eyes green?"

"Yes, they are."

When the server brought the pizza and cut it before us, we sat for an uncomfortable moment until he had gone. Then I silently gave thanks as imperceptibly as I could and cheerfully looked up at the pizza. But she had caught it.

"Oh. You're a Christian."

I nodded. "Are you?"

"How did you know?"

"I didn't, really," I stammered. "Well, your missionaries and everything."

"Yes, I am. Good. Isn't that nice. So, where do you go to church?"

"What slice would you like here?" I asked, reaching for the spatula.

"No. Here, let me do that." Deftly she took the utensil from me.

"Hey, you snatched that as if you did it every day. Afraid I'd spill it?"

"No. I'm good enough at that myself, thanks." She placed a slice on my paper plate and then took one for herself. "So, what church?"

"I'm not much for the organized church. I mean, I used to be, but not now." Waiting for her to eat first, I asked, "How about you?"

"I grew up in the assemblies, but now I go to an Presbyterian church." She cut a small piece of pizza and took it up with her fork. "So, you don't go anywhere? Are you one of those who are always looking?"

For a moment I watched her eat and then, as delicately as I could, lifted my slice with my hands, folded it down the center, and took a bite from its end. After taking a drink I replied, "Well, I kind of visit here and there."

"That's called *looking.*"

"Uh, yes. Yes, that's right. I guess I'm looking."

"A lot of people who do that do it perpetually, you know."

"Yes, I've heard that."

Rolling her eyes she exclaimed softly, "Oh, this is so good. Is yours?"

"Yeah, it's great. Very good."

"So, what kind of church are you looking for?"

"Uh, well, I think for a place where I could take my dogs."

After a moment she said, "A kennel? For just when you go to church?"

"Uh, no."

She swallowed. "You mean, you want to take your dogs to church?"

I nodded. "Um-hm."

Taking another bite with her fork, she asked, "That's, um. Well, what if everybody did that? I mean, the whole church would smell like dog."

"Yes, that's right. I imagine it would."

Then she stopped chewing, and asked quite deliberately, "Wait a minute. Why would you want to take your dogs to church?"

Feeling the very greenness of her inquisitive eyes, I answered, "Well, so they could experience corporate worship of God."

"Corporate worship of God."

"Yeah."

Blinking slowly, she said, "Animals don't worship God."

"Really? That's very interesting. How do you know that?"

"It makes sense. They don't have souls." Her irritation was not disguised. She had discovered that I was a box she perhaps did not want to open.

Chewing slowly, I looked at her for a moment. "What if I said they even have a spirit?"

"Then, I'd say you're nuts."

"Would you?" And when she hesitated I said, "Actually, in Genesis one, where it talks about living creatures, and it says, like, cattle and other animals—well, the original word for *creature* is *soul*. That means animals have a soul. And in Ecclesiastes three, I think maybe twenty or twenty-one, the term *spirit of the beast* means they have a spirit. And it's the same original word as used for the Spirit of God. So, it probably means a real soul and a real spirit, what do you think?"

"I think you don't need to be sarcastic."

I sighed. "You're right. I'm sorry."

Then she said, "What I mean is, dogs weren't made in the image of God."

In my most peaceful tone I replied, "Okay. I would concede that. But neither were the angels, who worship God a lot, I'd say."

"You think a dog would know it was in church?"

"Maybe not from a human perspective. I mean, I don't know. I don't expect a dog to know what I know, and I don't expect to know what a dog knows. But my dogs see me going to church, and I think they'd like to come along."

"Why?"

"Can I have another piece?" After she had placed it on my plate, I folded it and took a bite. Then I said, "To worship God, maybe. You know, as in *let everything that has breath praise the Lord.* Or maybe to sing."

"Sing? Oh, come on. Please."

"Dogs and wolves sing all the time."

"Yeah. For meat. And for something *else.*"

"How do you know?"

153

"Oh, come on. A wolf praising God. Come on."

"So, a donkey can carry Jesus but can't praise him?"

"And I suppose it's going to preach next."

"Well, Balaam's ass did a pretty good job of that."

"That's because God made it talk."

"No, no. It was very personal. She said basically *aren't I your ass and haven't I been faithful to you?* That's personal and emotional."

"God was just using the animal."

"I don't believe that. The angel said to Balaam something like *unless she had turned from me, I would have slain you and saved her alive.* That's basically God honoring the proper fear of an animal."

"Animals are not aware of God. They don't have God-awareness. Everybody knows that."

"Who knows that? Theologians? Ministers? It's funny they should know that and not know the Bible. It says *and when the ass saw the angel of the Lord.* Isn't that God-awareness? And maybe donkeys would like to go to church and sing to God with other creatures instead of having to go around saving the stupid prophets who whip them."

"Nice speech. But you're being a little naïve. Naïve and strange. I'm sorry, yes, *strange.*" She shook her head. "Okay. So, church will now smell like a barn."

"Well, cologne and perfume are pretty hard for *me* to take."

After a moment she said, "I don't use perfume."

And after moment of my own I said, "I noticed."

"You did?"

"Well, yes. I mean, I only noticed its absence."

Chapter 3

The next day, at the front of the class, I faced the silvered screen pulled down in front of the blackboard, and moved the dial on the old slide projector to raise the bright blank square to the screen's center. When satisfied I looked over at Judy on her folding chair. I guessed purple for the skirt and maybe peach for the top. These, along with her hair just nudging the shoulders, and gorgeous eyes, which at that distance even my memory couldn't paste in, presented a marvelous distraction. But there was no empty chair beside her and I would simply have to face the class. Relief came when she rose and walked toward me.

"You know," I whispered when she leaned close, "everything's digital now."

"I know, I know," she whispered back. "But actual slides are so much more fun. Isn't this fun?"

I nodded. "Sure. Yes."

"Oh, listen," she whispered even more softly, "if you could just try to stick to art today, I think that would be good."

"Right. Right, sure, okay," I whispered, and suddenly I was glad I had folded the cane and placed it out of sight beside the projector.

Then she said in full voice, "Now, class, please welcome Mr. Le Haley again." When the applause fell away she continued, "Well, Mr. Le Haley is going to show us slides of his paintings. He does lots of other types of paintings, I understand, but we're going to be seeing scenes today, and tomorrow, he'll show us his abstracts. We won't have questions today, so save those until Friday. Again, this is a note-taking exercise. So, busy, busy, okay?" With that she briefly touched my arm and walked toward her chair.

When I found myself stupidly staring after her and listening to the swish of her slacks, I abruptly turned to address the class. But before I said anything Judy called for a boy near the door to switch off the lights, so I simply reached over and pushed the first slide home. As the Black Moshannon marsh that spread across the screen elicited a positive response from most of the class, I squinted to see the light-green lily pads and deep-purple water. I knew that Terri was squinting, too.

With each of the twenty slides I tried to say something interesting about the location, the studio work, the painting itself, or some such and above all tried to sound happy. For some reason I occasionally turned to look toward Judy, whose presence seemed that of a policewoman in the dark. After finishing the show with an oil of Ricketts Glen, I turned again toward Judy, who then called for the lights. I then gave a short explanation of how I had gotten into art in the first place. I told how I had begun as an on-location artist, painting scenes of the park and its creek in Audubon and Haddon Heights in New Jersey. I sensed the fascination when I told how I affixed a paint box, easel and blank canvas to the rear rack of my bicycle for painting trips and how with this rig I was able to set up virtually anywhere, paint all day, and then transport everything, including the wet painting, neatly back to the studio. I told how, years later, the onset of low-vision made it practical to work only from photographs in the studio, where I could enlarge them and then work without glasses up close to the canvas.

When I ran out of things to say I announced that my talk was finished and then turned the class back to Judy. Suddenly I felt very tired and then, in a moment, nearly overcome with fatigue, as if a wave had come in from the ocean, lifted itself to a great height, crossed the beach, and fallen upon me. Even before Judy reached the center of the class to begin her usual prelunch announcements, I had collapsed onto a nearby chair. Although the sense of fatigue continued, the relief that came with being able to sit was so blissful that I closed my eyes.

On my return walk to the apartment, I forewent plans to make a reminiscent tour of the neighborhood and instead took the shortest route, along Herschel. Although I was beginning to feel better since the class, I could not deny that the incidence and severity of fatigue were apparently increasing. At the apartment I made a simple sandwich for lunch and then relaxed with oolong tea and cookies. Then I set the PDA's alarm for an hour and went to bed. Daytime naps always seemed to wreck my nighttime sleep, but avoiding them was becoming more difficult. I went to sleep quickly.

Upon awaking I tapped the PDA's screen with my finger to silence the alarm and then pushed the Off button. I was groggy but knew I had needed the rest. On the porch I raised the windows and settled in on the couch's old corduroy. I lifted the PDA to make a journal entry, but as it seemed unusually heavy, I lowered it again. Life was like that. You wanted to communicate, but the machinery for communicating seemed too heavy, so you just let it go. Sometimes even the voice seemed too heavy to lift.

With a couple of hours before Judy was to pick me up, I went to the kitchen and filled the water boiler to make tea. When the cycle finished I pressed and held the On button to bring the water to a true rolling boil and then filled the cup and stirred the tea to infuse the leaves. On the porch I pulled the plant stand close to the couch and set the cup on it. Settling in on the corduroy again, I looked out the window and breathed in the warm afternoon air. It seemed fresh and I thought of Judy's skin. I thought of her hair and her face, her eyes, her nose, her lips. And then I thought of the rest of her. I lifted the cup to taste the tea, but as it seemed unusually heavy, I lowered it again. Life was like that. You wanted to enjoy it, but the machinery for enjoying it seemed too heavy, so you just let it go.

At a little past four Judy pulled the small silver SUV up to the curb, and I stepped from the sidewalk and looked carefully through the glass of the passenger window to make sure it was she. First a hand waved and then the window dropped a few inches and I heard her voice. I got in, reached for the seat belt, and then looked at her.

"You know," I said whimsically, "you might just want to go into sorcery."

She chuckled. "What's that supposed to mean? Why?"

"I don't know. The hair, the sunglasses—kind of magical."

"Oh, good grief. You're nuts." She adjusted the glasses and then held her hands out, as if to accept applause. "They're Italian. Do you like them?"

"Yeah. They're really nice."

"Stunning?"

"Uh, yeah, I'd say that's the word."

"Thank you. They cost enough."

"Well, I think it's the woman that's made the sunglasses look good, not the other way around."

"Oh, you're nuts," she chortled. "You *read* that."

"No, I didn't."

Then she asked, "Where's your cane?"

"It feels a little clunky sometimes." And clicking the seat belt shut I added, "Maybe you could guide me tonight."

"Sure?"

"I'll be fine. Don't worry." As she accelerated and we moved out into the lane I observed, "You changed. Is that linen?"

"Yep. Hey, that's pretty good. You can see that?"

"Well, I've painted on enough of it. It just kind of looked like it. And I like the jeans."

"Thank you. Now we match."

I looked over at her hair and then back through the windshield. "So, does the shock of white mean you're independent?"

"Probably."

"And dangerous?"

"Probably."

"It looks nice. I like it."

"You tease a lot, don't you?"

"I guess I do."

"Actually," she said, "I've been thinking of going blond. What do you think?"

"I kind of like it the way it is. I was just wondering, that's all. You seem so independent. And most women color their hair, or at least I've been told they do."

"Well, I'm glad you like it."

"So, where are we going?"

"We're going to a seafood restaurant that I like. Is that okay?"

"Sure," I said. "I love seafood."

The trees of Riverside seemed to droop under their Spanish moss as we drove through the quiet neighborhood. Occasionally a street corner or a group of buildings would solicit my memory for images.

At length she remarked, "There is something profound about an old neighborhood."

"Yes."

"Anything look familiar?"

"Some things do," I replied. "A lot of the intersections are really familiar. It's like I was riding around on my bike after school. But some of it seems totally new to me, like it's been completely rebuilt or I simply don't remember it." I shrugged. "It doesn't matter."

"Come on, now. Don't be cynical. It's good to reminisce."

"I suppose."

"Maybe you can take a few new memories back to Philadelphia."

I looked down at her jeans and then out through my window. "Yes," I replied. "I could do that. That would be good."

"You know, memories are supposed to make you happy."

"Did you see the German Shepherd a few blocks back?"

"In the yard?"

"Uh-huh. It reminded me of a dog I used to have."

"Don't tell me. I only want to hear happy stories tonight. Is it happy?"

After a moment I answered, "Sure. Yeah."

"Good." And then, as if to change the subject, she retrieved a CD from the drop-down compartment and slid it into the player's slot. Adjusting the dial, she asked, "Do you like Bach?"

"Yes, sometimes," I replied. And then, leaning back until I barely felt the headrest, I closed my eyes to listen to the opening of the Brandenburg number one.

"Well," she said at length, "I think it's the greatest music."

"The Brandenburg concertos?"

"No, I mean Bach in general. And especially the Chaconne."

"Really. Who?"

"I think, Heifetz."

"What other music do you like?"

"Oh, the list is too long. Dvorak. I like Holst."

"What Holst do you like?"

"The St. Paul's Suite."

"You must like Vaughan Williams."

"Oh, please. He is *so* glorious."

"Isn't he? I love it, I just love the stuff."

And then she asked, "Who's *your* composer?"

"I like Vivaldi," I answered. "But I think Bruckner's my favorite."

"You like Bruckner?"

"*Like* is probably not the word," I replied.

"Oh."

"You're not a fan, I guess. You sound disappointed."

"Well," she said, "he's a little long, for me. And gloomy. Your Black Moshannons remind me of his symphonies."

"Is that good or bad?"

"I'm not sure, really. Beautiful. But, yeah, definitely gloomy."

"And Sibelius?" I asked, "I adore Sibelius."

"Same thing," she replied.

The small restaurant, squeezed humbly between a fabric shop and an insurance agency, presented itself unpretentiously as just another store front. In the window, next to a simple static neon sign, a magic-markered chart listed specials. The middle-aged woman who welcomed us led us to a booth with ancient leather upholstery and a checkered tablecloth. Judy knew her well enough to return her bright smile and nod, but not well enough to introduce me.

"This is charming," I remarked when the woman had gone to get water.

"Thank you. I thought you'd like it." And then, laying her menu down, she said, "Close your eyes and give me your hand."

I obeyed and felt raised dots. "Oh, Braille!"

"Yes," she said triumphantly, withdrawing her hands. "Salt, pepper, mustard."

"Wow, look at that, handicap-sensitive. That's great. That's the first time I've seen that in a restaurant."

I could see she was pleased, and I wished I could say it again. And although I wanted to feel her warm hands again, I simply looked into her eyes as she lifted the menu and began to read.

"So, what would you like?" she asked. And when I squinted at the selections she said, "Never mind. Here, I'll read it to you. It's a bit small."

"Yes. I don't need Braille, but a heavy font would help."

"Actually, they have a Braille menu. Isn't that cool?"

"Yeah. Neat."

"*Cool,*" she corrected.

"Sorry. I never used the term."

"Well, if you taught kids very long, you would."

"I'm glad it's well lit here," I said. "It's amazing how many restaurants are so dark you can't see a person's eyes."

"And whose eyes would you be wanting to see?"

The woman arrived with lemon-topped glasses of water. Quietly she took our orders and then left.

"So, you're a regular, huh?"

"Yes. I told you."

"This is Italian?"

"Very."

At length I asked, "Why do people relax after ordering in a restaurant?"

She removed the lemon slice from the rim of her glass. "Because they know they're going to have to wait."

"Possibly."

"Or maybe, in anticipation of fulfillment and enjoyment."

"Could be," I replied, adjusting my glasses.

As she took a sip of the water I watched her eyes until she had swallowed, trying to follow as much detail of her facial expression as I could. In the darkness I would need the detail to make the image more real. Others would actually see her face and appreciate its beauty, but I would need to remember it.

Lowering her voice, she said, "You're staring at me."

Then I remarked, "You know, you squint when you drink."

After a moment she replied, "Most people do, I think."

I nodded. "Yes."

"You squint pretty much all the time."

"Yes."

After taking another sip of water, she asked, "Do you eat out a lot?"

"Not too much. My dogs would miss me. I love to eat out, though."

"Alone?"

"What?"

"Do you eat out alone?"

"Oh. No. I mean, most of the time, I guess. Do you mean, do I go out with women?"

"Something like that."

"Sometimes. Not much."

After our salads had been left with us, she said, "Why don't you give thanks for both of us."

I replied, "Actually, why don't *you*?"

She hesitated, but then insisted, "No. I think, *you*."

So, we bowed our heads and I said quietly, "Dear God, we thank you for this food and for each other, in Jesus' name. Amen"

"There," she said, also quietly. "That's very nice. Thank you."

Then I asked, "So, why does Judy Morino teach the sixth grade and not do something else in life?"

"You ask big questions," she said. "Who knows? Doors open. Stuff leads to stuff."

"That sounds passive. You seem more aggressive than that."

She replied quietly, "You're probably right. I don't know. I was a music in college. Violin. Everything was going well. I got into my professor's strings group, went on tour, recorded with them, and then simply expected to finish college as a violin major and start applying for orchestra jobs. But one day . . . and it was just that simple . . . it was like I woke up from something and thought, well, I didn't want to spend the rest of my life practicing. And every day the practice room seemed to *decrease in size*. So, without thinking too much more about it, I switched my major to English, and here I am."

"And where's that?"

"Well, what am I supposed to say? I don't know. I'm here. I'm fifty-eight. I drive to work. I drive home. I've taught high-school music, English lit, and now the sixth grade. I vacation in the summer at the Jersey shore. Twice a year or more I visit my mom and dad in Mt. Holly. And that's what I do."

"But a happy fifty-eight?" I asked, reaching for the salt.

"I think so. A happy fifty-eight. I do my gardening after school. In the evenings I grade papers, which I hate. I've always hated it."

"But it's better than practicing?"

"Yes. And I've put in to retire early at sixty-two."

"What're you going to do then?"

"Good question. I think I'd like to retire to Cape May. I'd be close to my parents and a not-too-hot sun. I could walk the beach every morning. Watch the sun come up and go down. Take an occasional trip into Philadelphia, spend the day shopping, sit in Rittenhouse Square, walk down to Chinatown. Or sometimes just drive up along the shoreline and shop the boardwalks. I love seafood, and I love the salt air. I think I just want to spend the rest of my life in the salt air."

"That's a pretty simple list. I hope you get it."

Then her eyes closed a little. "I think I'd add just one thing to it. I've always wanted to sell jewelry. You know, like, artistic silver jewelry?"

"You mean, in a store?"

She shook her head. "No. As a vendor. A sidewalk vendor. In Cape May. I could have cases set out on a table and an umbrella and chair. I've always wanted to do that. What do you think?"

"I don't know. It seems reasonable. But maybe Cape May has zoning laws and things that would make it impossible. Other than that, maybe, I guess."

"What zoning laws? I've *bought* from vendors there."

"Yeah. Well, that certainly sounds workable, to me. I wish you luck."

"You think it's feasible?"

"Yes. Actually, that sounds like a beautiful life, very simple, unpretentious, true."

Momentarily she said, "Is that how you see me?"

"Yes. I think so. Some people might say, a little *odd*, but I wouldn't worry about it."

"Odd?"

"A little, I think. Some people might see you that way. You know, I mean, you're different."

"How do you see me as different?"

"I don't know. A little flamboyant. More like, artistic."

Then she laughed, as if at herself, and said, "I don't know why I asked you. You're the one who wants dogs to go to church, and you think I'm the one who's different?"

"I think so, yeah. You seem to have an oddness about you, but in a positive way, I think."

The salad plates were removed and very hot platters of seafood were placed before us. As we moved aside the small porcelain cups of tartar and other sauces and coleslaw, little scenes of Italy could be seen on the edges of the plates.

"Aren't they cute?" she said. "I was hoping you could see them."

"Yes, they are. And the food. This is wonderful. Why does fried food have such power over me? This is really nice."

"You'll love it."

"Yeah. It'll probably kill me. I love fried food, especially shrimp and scallops."

"Most men do," she returned. Then, reaching across with her fork, she said, "Here take a bite of this." When I taken it she withdrew the fork slowly. "Is that crab cake or what—incredible, isn't it?"

"You're right, it's very good."

"Better than good," she corrected.

"Okay, better than good. Would you like to try some of mine?"

"Yes, I would, thank you." And she took two shrimp from my plate with her fingers.

"This is a very comfortable place," I observed. "And discreet, like a rendezvous place."

"So, you know what a rendezvous place is like? *How* do you know?"

"Good question. Movies, probably," I replied. "So, what are you doing with music now?"

"Well, I still play the violin and I've added the viola. I see a few private students a week. Once a month I play quartets with musicians I know. And I've done some composing."

"Do you play piano?"

"Yes."

"Sing?"

"Yes. Actually, I'm sort of on a search for new pieces to sing. I'm very tired of my Sixties stuff. You don't write, do you?"

"Only a little."

"I'm looking for at least new words, so I can set them to music."

I said dubiously, "I have one poem that might work. It's strictly old school, though. I wrote it when I was younger. You'd probably scrap it. It's kind of trite."

"How does it go?"

I put down my fork. "*Your love is like the summer, with sunshine all around. Your love is like the autumn, with soft leaves falling down. Your love is like the winter, with snowflakes in the air. Your love is like the springtime, with flowers everywhere.* And then, the second part is *Your love is like the daytime, with glory in its eyes. Your love is like the evening, with honey in its cries. Your love is like the night time, with stars that fill the blue. Your love is like the morning, with kisses all brand new.*" I picked up my fork. "It's a little trite, I think. I composed it over about a week's time, every day on my bike ride into work. That was a long time ago."

"Yeah, it seems a little trite, but I like trite things sometimes. And besides, we shouldn't let modernity define us, right?"

I was charmed, and replied, "I agree."

"Good."

And then I added, "I have always wanted to change the word *brand* in the last line to one less mundane. I guess it doesn't matter."

"Everything matters," she retorted defensively.

"I've heard that."

"Doesn't it?"

"Some of it sure seems not to. Sometimes all of it seems not to."

With a faint shake of her head, she said, "Okay. So, now you're going to tell me you think nothing matters. As a Christian, how can you have an intentional God and have nothing matter, tell me that?"

"No, I think you're right. It does matter. And I imagine, if any of it matters, it all must. The problem is that it seems not to."

"But you can't let the disparity between what God knows and what you know paralyze you. Otherwise, life will destroy you. Or you'll self-destruct."

"I've heard that too. Would you like a scallop?"

Momentarily she reached across and pushed her fork into one of the scallops on my plate. After cutting it in half on her own plate, she put a piece into her mouth. While she chewed I watched her for a response, but she was silent.

"So," I asked, I suppose to change the subject, "are you Italian?"

"Half," she replied. "My grandfather grew up in Dugenta. I was there when I went to Europe after college. He always said things never changed there, or at least not as fast as they did here. So, he told me that when I got to Dugenta I should look for the bullet holes in the town wall where people had been executed. I did and they were still there."

"Did you like Europe?"

She closed her eyes and whispered, "Yes."

"I read that a lot of Americans are retiring to Italy."

"I've thought about it. I think I could do that, I really do. For me, visiting Italy was like turning on the light. There's an incredible atmosphere of sunshine and beautiful things. The culture's a little frenetic sometimes, but I think I could make the trade."

Then I asked, "Were you ever married?" And when she did not respond but drew her breath slowly, I said, "Sorry."

She shook her head. "No, I've never been married. Have you?"

I shook my head, also. "So, why not? You look like you've certainly had suitors."

"*Look like*? What is that supposed to mean?"

"I guess it means I think you're very nice to look at. You're talented, intelligent, successful, and beautiful, anyone can see that. You must have had a lot of men after you."

"Are you always adding things up, analyzing everything and adding it up?"

"It's a fault. Sorry."

"I mean, things would add up about *your* life, right?"

I shook my head. "No. Sorry."

Then she said, "There have been a few men. And a couple of times, I was close to saying yes. I just didn't say it."

"Why?"

"Do I have to have a reason?"

"No. I was just curious."

Then she asked, "What about you?"

"I don't know." I scratched the side of my nose. "It never worked out. I don't know."

"Did you ever ask anyone?"

"No."

"Why?"

"You ask big questions," I said. And after she didn't reply, I said, "I don't quite know why."

"Were you waiting to fall in love?"

Her voice and her eyes were kind, or at least my mind was telling me so. I looked at her for a moment and then answered, "No, I can't honestly say that. I think I fall in love all the time."

Chapter 4

At noon the next day I sat at the side of the class and waited for Judy to close the day's activities and dismiss the fidgeting students. It seemed, as I reflected, that the slide show of my abstracts had gone well and that I had not said anything she might call weird or that might have hurt anyone's feelings, so I could relax. I followed her movements as she forced a drawer of her desk closed and then stood to address the class. When she straightened her back and lifted her chin ever so slightly to prepare to speak, the whole form, from the silvered hair to the electric black straps of the sandals, seemed a perfectly matched battery. Even at that distance I found her irresistibly lovely, and I wondered why looking at beautiful things had to be so refreshing.

She spoke in the clear voice of someone who had learned to reach every ear with every word. "Tomorrow will be Mr. Le Haley's last day with us. He'll be coming for just a question-and-answer session to wrap up his visit. So it will be a good time to ask any other questions you might have. Write all your questions down tonight and bring them with you to class. Have a good afternoon and

I'll see you tomorrow." Then she motioned to the boy on the back row who had tended the lights, and he opened the door and with his foot pushed its prop against the floor.

As the classroom emptied I shut off the projector and began placing my slides into their box. Occasionally I glanced over to Judy, who was quietly occupied with straightening up the top of her desk. I was struck by how easily her beauty paled that of the paintings I had just shown in the slides.

"Another teacher's planning afternoon?" I asked.

She forced a drawer closed in the desk and looked up. "Yes."

"You like old things, don't you?"

Her answer was defiant. "Yes, I do."

"The drawers on a new metal desk would close at a touch."

She retrieved a wayward pen and stuck it into a ceramic holder. "This desk is older than I am. I rescued it from the school trash and cleaned it up with ammonia and water. I thought about refinishing it, but I kind of liked all the marks."

"You can soap the drawers."

"I know," she sighed. "I just keep forgetting to bring it in. Listen, I brought some things for a picnic. Would you like to join me?"

"Yes," I answered softly, and then, "Where?"

"Just down the street, by the library."

"Oh yes, I used to play there. I used to ride my bike there after going to the candy store."

"Uh-huh. Well, I thought we could try to find a spot by the creek."

I nodded eagerly. "Fine."

"Okay," she said, "you finish up with your slides and I'll change."

Half an hour later we spread a wool army blanket not far from the park's creek and unpacked her lunch basket. Everything was there, not for one person, but for two. She seemed very comfortable as she unwrapped and handed me one of the sandwiches. I was comfortable, too. The tall pines swaying above shaded us from the noon sun. I waved away a spring fly, unscrewed the top from the bottle of water she had handed me, and listened to the sounds of a softball game not far away. Memories began to flood my mind, so many memories of so long ago. Judy's voice brought me back.

"The kids liked your abstracts," she said cheerily.

I watched her take a sip from her bottle of water. She seemed to be on display somehow, and I took in her T-shirt and shorts, her legs. Looking at the shorts, I asked, "Are those black?"

"Navy blue," she answered.

Following the movements of her body as she brushed a gnat from her leg and then reached for a potato chip, I marveled at the apparent ease with which nature expressed beauty. How I had labored to produce beautiful things. I had spent many of the years and much of the energy of my adult life trying to express beauty in paint, often through the employment of elaborately concocted imagery; and yet here, in one brief moment, and apparently effortlessly, nature, as if to show me how it was done, was expressing it before me in the simple movements of this woman. I looked away from her, toward the softball field and the houses beyond.

"Is there still a candy store over there," I asked, "two or three blocks up from the school?"

"I never go that way," she replied.

"Strange, the things that never leave you."

"I know. The brain's a weird machine."

"It is. What do you remember?"

"About being a kid?"

"Yeah. What are your best memories?"

She sighed, gently clasping her elbow. "I don't know. Memories are so warped. I suppose I like remembering the freshness of just being young. My skin was fresh. My hair was fresh. Even the air was fresh, and the water. I know it wasn't, but I remember it that way. I loved riding bikes and going on adventures with my sisters. To ride all the way around the block was an achievement. And I loved having fun—fun itself. I lived it. I possessed it like it was something tangible. There was a little path behind our house that my sisters and I called the Indian Path. You can't even see it today, it's just part of the neighbor's yard, and yet it was so important to us." She looked away and was silent.

"What else?"

"I remember going to girls camp, making new friends, and writing letters to them when I got home. I'm very bad at writing letters. It's not my thing, so I wasn't exactly a pen pal. But I loved the adventure of it all. I remember Christian youth groups in high school. I guess they were probably pretty boring, but they seemed exciting at the time, and I think I made the most of them. And then, I don't know, for the rest, I just tried to get my school work done on time and, I guess, prepare for college." She rolled her eyes and added, "I was not very organized."

"But you had a vision of generally how things were going to unfold?"

"Oh, I think my vision then was probably as warped as my memory is now."

"Actually, your memory sounds really lucid, objective, to me. Did you go to a Christian school."

"No. Public."

I nodded.

"I remember reading a lot," she continued. "For me, a book was an adventure, an adventure filled with incredible emotion. It was thrilling, absolutely thrilling to get a new book to read."

"You keep using that word."

"Which?"

"*Adventure.*"

She nodded, smiling. "Yes. *Adventure.*"

"A synonym for *life*?"

"I suppose," she replied. "Anyway, I read all the time. Just about every moment, I had a book in my hand. My glasses were really thick. Couldn't wait to get contacts. Yep, *so ugly*, I thought. My mother said I was ruining my eyes, and I believed her, but still kept reading. And then, the orchestra, that was another sphere entirely. I loved it. I loved it while it was happening. The experience was real to me, not like so much of life, where you don't even know what's happening. I knew I loved it. I savored all of it."

"Boyfriends?"

She nodded. "A few. They never wanted to just have fun, at least not clean fun. They always had to get serious. You had to wear their class ring. Goofy stuff. Possession. Control. But all I really wanted was adventure and fun, to enjoy life. Yes, I think that's what I remember most. Just the freshness of everything."

"Sounds idyllic."

As if awaking, she said, "Uh-huh. Yeah, that's probably the word. Were you a reader?"

"Yes."

"Who did you read?"

"I don't know. Conrad, London, and later, Tolstoy, Dostoyevsky. I loved Steinbeck."

"You liked adventure?"

I shrugged. "I guess I did. My bookshelf says I did. But I think I was looking for some other than excitement. Isolation, maybe."

"You're not supposed to look for isolation. Accept it, maybe, but not look for it."

"You sound pretty sure about that."

She dropped her gaze. "No. No, I'm not. Were you a loner?"

"No, I had a few friends. I was fairly normal, I think."

"What makes me doubt that?"

"Why?"

"Well, you think animals can preach. You think they might like to—" she broke off, nodding vigorously for emphasis, "go to church. You paint beautiful landscapes and seascapes, but with no people in them. And strange abstracts with multiple moons and symbols, but again, no people.

I mean, they're nice, colorful, interesting—but strange. So, a normal childhood? I don't think so."

"Maybe it was a little strange. Maybe what did it was all that licorice from the candy store."

She laughed. "You liked licorice, too?"

"I did, I did. Yep. And just about every other kind of candy. Spearmint—ah, spearmint. Oh, yeah, too much candy, I think. Spearmint, peppermint, licorice, hot candy, sour candy, chocolate. You name it, and I ate it."

"Were you overweight?"

"No," I laughed. "I was always skinny. Probably from all the exercise I got. My family were all thin. I did get a little heavy on steroids a few years ago, but then lost it on the new meds."

"But, so, no *bad* memories?"

I looked toward the creek. "It's funny how many faces there seem to be in my memories." I laughed softly. "I turned in a dog to the city shelter once. I had to do it, at least it seemed that way at the time. There wasn't much else I could do. He was a stray that had attached himself to me. But he was aggressive, and the neighbors, cute little kids, were frightened of him. And he was a really fearsome dog. Anyway, I turned him in. I called the city and they sent someone out to get him. And I helped to capture him, on my patio, no less, where he had set himself up as my protector, where he felt safe, I'm sure. Yeah . . . I see his face a lot."

"How? Like in dreams?"

"Not so much in dreams. A little bit, but not so much. Usually, just as I'm thinking to myself, you know, through the day, at different times. I see his face, the way he looked at me when I betrayed him."

"Betrayed?"

"Yes."

"But," she reasoned, "if it couldn't have been helped?"

"He was still betrayed. And I still see his face."

She shook her head. "You keep doing that, your perspective. You keep referring to animals as if they were human, like they had a sense of honor and betrayal. I guess, they might have a *sense* of honor. I mean, okay, I can see that. But they don't *think* it. They can't grasp it as an idea. They don't think like humans. They're instinctive creatures."

"And then I had a dog put to sleep. She was old and very sick. She had tumors in her head. She was close to being in constant pain, the doctor said, so it wasn't avoidable. I held her face in my hands, so very gently, and whispered to her to calm her as the doctor put her to sleep. And I felt, I *knew* she was trusting me as she collapsed and died in my hands."

"And you blame yourself?"

"I'm afraid so."

She was incredulous. "For what?"

"I don't know. Just being the agent, I suppose."

"The usher, huh?"

"Yes."

"Well, that's really stupid, if I have to say it. I can see you're really hurt. I'm sorry. But you should think about the implications. I mean, that condemns all of us. We all have to be an agent, an usher, sometime. We all have pets that we end up having to put to sleep. They don't live that long.

They get sick and live in pain. You have to put them to sleep. It's a mercy. It's good, it's not bad."

"I know. You're right."

She sighed. "You've done a lot of good for dogs, though, right? You must have. And for other animals, too. Do you see their faces?"

"Not really. I mean, I remember them, but it's not the same."

After a moment she said, "There's such a thing as healing, you know."

"That's true."

"Some people can't do it, though. They just can't seem to forgive themselves for things they've done."

"It's not quite that simple, I think."

"Well, it is, I think," she returned. "It is that simple. They forgive you. You forgive yourself. That's what forgiveness is. It just erases everything, and you go on with your life."

"Yeah," I replied, again looking toward the creek. "That's what people say. But for me, it just doesn't seem to be that simple. You know, along that creek there, I forget where, somewhere shallow, I remember, I used to chase the tiny fish with a can, trying to catch them. My friend and I would just pull up by the creek, leave our bikes, and go walking along the muddy sand, scooping into the water with our cans or jars. We simply hunted them, for no reason at all, except for entertainment, because we were bored on a Saturday afternoon. Imagine being a little fish or frog, with a life all your own in your little water world, and having a giant, a monster, two of them, suddenly splash into that world and come after you to possess you and, you know, to take away your life. Imagine it. And all of it, simply because the monsters were tired of riding their bikes and were bored on a Saturday afternoon. . . . No, we had no idea why we were doing it. Just for the fun of it, to catch them."

Then she asked, "Did you ever hurt things, on purpose?"

"No, of course not. I did shoot a pigeon with a slingshot once, when I was a kid. But he got away, and I never did it again. I felt really ashamed somehow. It's funny, but it was a powerful hunting slingshot—I don't know why I had wanted one. I was a high-energy kid, always riding a bike and climbing trees. But anyway, I remember that feeling of being ashamed. I don't know where it came from."

"Okay, so, have you forgiven yourself for that?"

I shook my head.

"So, you can't just go on with your life?"

I shrugged, but didn't answer.

"That's not really healthy, you know."

"I know."

"But why?" she asked. "Exactly *why* can't you forgive yourself?"

I wanted so much to please her, to give the answers that would satisfy her. But somehow I knew that I would not be able to provide those answers. Life is like that, it denies you things. Finally I answered, "I don't know. I think, maybe, because of reality."

"You know, you lose me sometimes. What . . . what do you mean by *reality*?"

"Well, I mean, you can ask someone's forgiveness, but you can't actually remove the wrong itself. It happened. And the person was hurt. That's the reality of it."

"Yes, but once that person forgives you, you don't brood about it, you let it go. You don't have anxiety about the wrong when you remember it. Right?"

"That's the theory," I acknowledged. "But I can't seem to make it work."

"Can't or won't?"

"I don't know." I shook my head. "Besides, how do you ask the forgiveness of someone who is dead?"

"If they're dead, they don't care," she said. "They're in the next world."

"What difference does that make?"

"It means they don't care anymore."

"How do you know that?"

She waved a gnat from her cheek, then looked at me. "I guess, I don't. . . . Are we talking about the dog?"

"Uh, yeah, I guess."

"Or about everything you've ever hurt?"

I shook my head. "I'm not sure."

Scratching under her eye, she asked, "But what about the healing?"

"Yeah. Time's supposed to do that, isn't it? I can't seem to make that work either."

Toward the middle of the afternoon we closed up the basket, folded the blanket, and returned to the school. When Judy left me in the main foyer and went to change out of her shorts and close her classroom, I stepped into the auditorium and took a seat on the back row. It seemed that no one else was there. I was not tired from the walk, but somehow the interior atmosphere, like ether, seduced me, and I found myself pushing against the back of the seat to make it recline. But it did not yield and I was forced to pay attention as the curtain before my memory opened and I saw on its stage the faces of friends, classmates, teachers and girls from my years at the school, friends I had survived with, classmates I had known but not been close to, teachers I had feared and listened to, girls I had fallen in love with. I recalled the festivals that had seemed so beautifully to demarcate and illustrate the seasons. Halloween, with its mythology of weird creatures and its mystical moon. Thanksgiving, with its fantasy of family and history. Christmas, with its menagerie of the extended Christian world. Easter, with its efflorescence of new life.

But suddenly this curtain seemed to close, and I heard the faint sound of a piano being played and then of someone singing with it. It was Judy's voice, possibly from behind the curtain on the stage. I went to the front of the auditorium, mounted the steps, and pushed the curtain open from the side, just enough to see. The light was quite dim and I could just see the outline of her hair and shoulders and the oval of her face as she sat at the keys of a baby grand. In a pleasant voice, a good voice, a singing voice, she was trying a melody with the first stanza of the poem. I didn't approach but held the curtain open and watched her on the unlit stage and listened. Oh, the power of beauty. I was mesmerized. But when you're being put under what you perceive to be a good spell you don't resist. You simply let it happen. You enjoy the moment.

When she stopped I said, "You know, I would've loved having you for a teacher. I would have come to school just to sit in your class."

"Here?"

"Um-hm. That would have been very nice."

Gently she pulled the keyboard cover down, then after a moment rose, and walked toward me. As she stepped through the opening she asked, "So, what dreams did you dream when you were here?"

I released the curtain, descended the steps after her, and walked with her up the aisle to the back of the auditorium. Once outside, on the front steps of the school, I replied, "Well, there was a girl in the fifth grade, with blond hair and very, very beautiful eyes. Every day her father drove her to school in a new Cadillac. I wondered how to tell a rich girl that I loved her. So, I didn't tell her. Then, in the sixth grade there was a very tall girl, with red hair, and again, lovely eyes. I loved her too, but the summer came, and I never told her. Those were my dreams."

At length she said, "You still dream, I hope."

"Yes," I replied. "Yes, I do."

Then we both looked away, as if to change the subject.

"Listen," she said, "I wish we could have dinner tonight, but I have to go to another school, a PTA meeting. I tried to get out of it. Sorry."

"A long meeting?"

"Yeah, unfortunately. Probably a couple hours or more. You wouldn't want to come, trust me. Sorry."

I shook my head. "No, that's okay. I'll see you tomorrow. . . . I will miss you, though."

"Yes," she replied softly.

"You look very nice. Kind of dressed up."

She shrugged. "It's just a skirt."

"I won't guess the color."

"Turquoise."

"Huh. I would've been wrong. But it looks nice."

"Thanks. I had a good time this afternoon. It was good to talk."

"Yes."

After a moment she said, "Can I take you home? I'll be going that way."

"Sure. Yeah, thanks."

In the early evening, I sat on the porch, the rocking chair creaking beneath me. I had fried a piece of fish from the freezer for dinner, and the taste of it was still in my mouth as I sipped hot oolong and smelled the orange blossom-scented air as it drifted in from the yard. The tea's temperature still must drop considerably before I could enjoy its distinctive flavor and hope to overcome the taste from the fish. The fig bars I had waiting would help.

Placing the cup on a plant stand beside my chair, I recalled going fishing with my older brother Michael when I was ten. We had gone on a Saturday to fish from the river wall at the end of King Street. We knew that the St. Johns was dirty at that place, but we didn't care, for Michael loved fishing and would try to catch something anywhere there was water. He was good at fishing. I was a tag-along. Baiting our hooks with cheap shrimp from the grocery, we cast out as far as we could and then watched the bobbers for a dip. Michael said it was going to be a good day. He caught many fish. I caught only one, although I tried to catch more. It was a small drumfish. After reeling it in, I ripped the hook from its mouth and tossed it onto the grass beside the concrete wall. It flipped and wiggled in the hot summer air, it's sides heaving, its black drumfish mark rising and falling. I was only curious, for it was just a fish, and fish were nothing. I loaded the hook with more bait, straightened the line at the rod's tip, placed a thumb on the line in the reel, clicked the drag off, and then pulled back and cast out for another try. After the splash, I watched the bobber for a moment and then turned around to look at my fish on the grass. First I looked at the mark, then at the eye, and then somehow into the face of the dying drumfish. It was not until much later in my life that I knew the fish had been looking back at me.

When I sensed the tea had cooled to within the right range I lifted the cup again. With the new taste of fig bars and Black Dragon tea on my palate, I thought of Tai Ping, Ragnar, and Sono. Full of their dinner, they would be lounging along the rug in the dining room. Catherine would come over again, just before ten, let them out to the yard, and then close them in for the night. And they would sleep, although not peacefully, for they would be waiting for me to return. It would be the same as the last time I had to leave them. On my return Catherine had told me of their restlessness, their melancholy, their pining. And what else should they do? For I had looked into their faces, and they had looked into mine, and the bond would never be broken. I sipped the tea and breathed the evening air. Yes, soon they would sleep for the night. They would have each other for company, but they would be alone.

Chapter 5

Standing before the class the next day, I put my hands in my pockets, as I had left the cane folded on Judy's desk. She had given the introduction for this last session and retired to her usual spot as observer. It was to be a short session simply for answering questions and wrapping up the week's visit. As usual a low hum of anticipation pervaded the classroom. For some reason, I looked over at Judy and, as much as I could, into the blur that was her face. Perhaps I looked too long, for suddenly the general hum changed to an obvious silence. I dropped my gaze and looked out over the class.

"So, uh, does anyone have a question?" I asked in a low voice, and when a boy in the third row raised a hand I motioned in his direction.

"Do you like photography?" he asked.

"Uh, yes, I do. Very much." Then through an awkward silence I heard Judy's voice of suggestive encouragement.

"Tell us something about photography, Mr. Le Haley."

Looking toward her, I muttered, "Uh, yes." Then somehow I had the sense to look back at the boy. "Well, it's a wonderful way to do art," I said. "Actually the photography world has changed over the last few years and is now virtually all digital. With digital cameras you can take as many pictures as you want with almost no cost for the actual picture. Printing can cost a lot, but you don't actually ever have to print the pictures. You can just view them on a computer and even email them. When my vision gets worse I'll probably just do photography all the time. Working with pictures on a computer screen is really easy for me, because the light comes from behind the picture and makes it glow."

Then I pointed toward the student next to him, who had raised her hand prematurely.

"I want to be an artist, Mr. Le Haley," she said, "but I can't draw. Even my mom says I really stink."

The girl didn't seem to mind the laughter that followed, and I was grateful for the time it gave me. "Well, actually," I said, "a lot of really good artists don't draw well at all. I mean, that sounds crazy, but it's true. Drawing isn't everything. Drawing is a skill that you learn. I mean, you can always practice and learn to draw better. But art is more about what you are inside, the way you think and look at things. Even if you can't draw well, you can make beautiful things. If you think like an artist, you *are* an artist."

"Don't you have to go to art school?" she asked.

"Not really," I replied. "Going to art school can be good for learning the tools and materials used in doing art, and even learning skills like drawing and working with paint. You can learn faster in art school than by just teaching yourself, because you're doing assignments and working with teachers and other students. But art is one of those things you can do without having to go to school to learn it. It's not like medicine or law, where you have to learn zillions of rules and procedures. I mean, if a doctor does something wrong, the patient can die. But if an artist paints something wrong, nobody's going to die, and painting something wrong can sometimes make it look better. You can pretty much teach yourself in art. There are tons of books on drawing and art materials. A lot of the world's great artists were, for the most part, self-taught. If you want to be an art teacher, though, you'll probably have to go to school and get a degree in art. But everybody's different, and I think you have to ask yourself what you want to do with art, how fast you want to learn it, things like that."

Then a boy near the back of the room asked, "Do you paint naked people?"

A titter of laugher arose, so I waited again and then said, "Uh, well, yes, I *have*. Uh, a person without clothes is just one thing to paint. As an artist you can paint anything you want. If a picture I hang on the wall bothers somebody, well, I just take it down. I mean, I don't want to offend anybody. I've found that when a person is offended, most of the time it means their feelings are hurt. And I don't want to hurt anybody's feelings. So, I think artists should feel free to paint what they want, but they should be careful where they show it."

Then a girl near me, who had said nothing during the other sessions that week, asked, "I like faces. Do some artists paint just faces?"

"Yes, they do. Paul Klee was a famous artist who did a lot of faces. And I know a very good artist, named Laura Pritchard, who does tons of faces. Really gorgeous. So, yeah, faces. You can do *just* faces, if you want. You can specialize in them and discover all kinds of ways of doing them. It's been said that you can see the whole world in someone's face."

She grinned delightedly at this and said, "I draw faces."

"Good. What do you draw with?"

"My mom has pastels."

"Good. Wonderful."

Then a boy with a shaved head asked, "Do artists make a lot of money?"

"No, unfortunately. Very few painters make a good living. Most have to have a regular job to support them in their art. I have a regular job, editing manuscripts at a medical school. My art is in a very good gallery in Philadelphia and they've sold a lot of my paintings over the years, but the money I make from paintings has never been enough to live on. Not even close. It's been enough to pay for art supplies, but that's all."

"But some artists get rich," he insisted.

"Well, it has happened, that's true, but not to very many. The things I've read say that, at least in America, virtually all artists have to have a regular job to support themselves. It's too bad, but that's just the way it is. You can only sell what people are interested in, and most Americans aren't interested in paintings." At his obvious dejection I added, "Art's more like something you love to do than something you make a lot of money doing. Art's more like something you need to do because of the way you think. You think in terms of images and making beautiful things. That's everything to an artist. Even working with the materials is wonderful. The paint, the canvas, the wood strips, the way it all goes together. Just all of it, the whole process of making a work of art. There's something wonderful and beautiful about just making beautiful things."

Although I felt satisfied with my explanation, I also sensed that it had not been entirely necessary and that some in the class, perhaps many, knew better than I how to discern the qualitative among the quantitative. When suddenly, ghostily, Judy appeared at my side I just stood there, hands in pockets, feeling quite stupid, looking back and forth from her to the class. Finally I realized that she was there to close the session, so I smiled and tipped my head toward her and then toward the class, as if to bow.

"Thank you, Mr. Le Haley. We are all very glad you could come to our school and be with us this week. We've learned a lot about art and low vision. We know it was a long way for you to come, and we wish you a good, safe trip back to Philadelphia. And, Mr. Le Haley, we all just loved your paintings. Thank you again." Immediately she began to clap her hands, as did the class.

Embarrassed, I grinned and waved to the class as they clapped. When the applause ended Judy presented her hand for me to shake and after that patted me on the shoulder and leaned close and spoke to me softly, as if to a child.

"It's okay," she said reassuringly. "You can go now."

So, I turned, snatched the cane from the edge of her desk, took the center aisle and left the classroom. As the door closed behind me I could hear her giving further instructions to the class.

Instead of taking Herschel back to the apartment, I turned at James and walked down the hill to St. Johns Avenue, following the route I used to take on my way home from school. I would drag my lunch box along the top of the low brick fence to see if I could wear its metal side through. But I never succeeded and eventually the metal rusted. At St. Johns I turned left and walked past King Street and then the hospital, where I used to roller skate, ride my bike, and watch the nuns as they occasionally strolled the grounds. Then I turned left, climbed the hill to Herschel, and returned to the apartment.

I was very tired. The fatigue from the MS seemed suddenly especially malicious, so that raising the windows on the porch was like lifting barbells. In the bedroom I fluffed the pillow and lay down for a nap. The paper-covered ceiling seemed dingy as I looked up at it, although dinginess was a condition I could no longer honestly discern. Everything seemed dingy, if it existed at all. Closing my eyes, I thought of Judy's silvered hair, her face, her eyes, and in my mind I painted them as bright and beautiful.

I awoke just after three and sat up. The bedroom was uncomfortably warm, and the midafternoon air was motionless. I rubbed my face, then massaged the area just above my eyes. In a brief dream I had seen Helga running, her ears back, her tail stretched out.

Early in the evening I opened the PDA's Medical folder, tapped on the Injections file, and scrolled to check which leg I had injected the previous Friday. I loosened my belt, pushed my jeans down, and alcohol-swabbed my left thigh. When I had removed the plastic cap from the syringe and twisted the needle onto it, I bulged the thigh muscle with my left hand and drove the needle home with my right. Pressing the plunger, I relaxed pressure on the muscle to allow room for the injection fluid. When the injection was complete I extracted and capped the needle, twisted it from the syringe, and dropped it into the red safety box for sharps.

It was after seven when Judy tapped on the screen door. "Sorry I couldn't come sooner," she said. "Fridays are always hectic and I had to go home after school."

"Oh, sure, sure," I returned cheerily. "I'm just glad you came. Come on in. I'm sorry you had to go home. You've got to be tired. Come on, sit down. I'll make some tea." Leaving to put the water on, I heard her sigh as she sat on the couch. From the kitchen I said, "You've pulled your hair back. It looks good."

"Thanks. I wear it this way sometimes. Listen, you didn't know, but the kids all made drawings for you. It was part of their homework. We can both take a look at them, if you want."

So, with tea and cookies we sat in the warm evening and remarked on the orange blossoms and spoke of the class, the slides, the sessions of the week that had passed. The atmosphere was muggy and still, and even on oscillation the old fan seemed ineffective. When she pulled the folder of drawings from her satchel and handed it to me, I placed it between us on the couch and turned the cover to show the first picture.

"I told them they could use what they wanted," she said. "Some of these are just in pencil."

"Pencil's a neat medium," I replied. "I just can't see it anymore, that's all. At least, not much. Low contrast."

"Listen, I'm sorry we didn't have a party for you. I sort of guessed you didn't care for ceremony, so I decided just to skip it. Were you okay with that?"

"Sure I was. That was fine. Actually, I liked everything just the way you did it. You were very cordial, I thought. And the kids were great."

"I'm glad you thought so."

"Well, let's see these things," I said and began turning the drawings over. "We have birds, fish, clouds, even two abstracts. They're all beautiful. Oh, and this must be from the girl who asked about faces." I held it close to read the name at the bottom.

"Jenna."

"Yeah, I see," I said. "Jenna. Yeah. Sorry. I didn't get their names very well, did I?"

"No."

"Yeah. Sorry."

"It's supposed to be you."

"Yes, I see that. Yes. Thanks." I turned the drawing over and picked up another. "I'll have to write them a thank you note for having me and for all these drawings. Tell them thanks for me, but I'll write them a note myself when I get home."

Nodding, she said, "That would be good."

"Who did this one? There's no name." The picture, of a sleeping dog, had been drawn entirely in heavy black crayon.

"Terri did it. She wrote on the back. Here, I'll read it. *Dear Mr. Le Haley. I don't know what your dogs look like but you must like them if you have three of them.*"

"Can she see color at all?"

"Not much. She can't even see pencil."

I chuckled. "Yeah, I know. Pencil's tough, no contrast."

"She has to do her school work with a dark pen. But she gets it done."

"Right."

Momentarily she said, "Come on, don't be sad."

"I'm not sad. It was a good week. Nice kids."

"Um-hm. Well, you made quite an impression on them, it seems. I have a number of them now who want to be artists." She shook her head. "Who knows?"

"Yes. Right. Who knows?" I closed the folder. "Well, I'll write the class a letter when I get home and thank them. They were really polite and it was a good week."

"Maybe individual letters, if you have time?"

"Oh, uh, yeah. Yeah, that's right. Good. Sure. I'll have time. I'll do that." The light from the tall floor lamp took my attention to her hair, and I followed the glow to where it disappeared in the loosely clasped ponytail. "I'll miss them."

"You could always come back next spring," she ventured.

Trying to follow the curve of her ear, I suggested, "Maybe you should get another act. A career person maybe. Someone in business. You know, someone who could tell them how to get rich."

"Or maybe someone just a little happier."

"A clown."

"Yes," she chuckled. "Yes, maybe a clown." And then, when I grinned, she said, "You don't smile much. it looks good. You should smile more. Definitely." Leaning closer, she asked, "Did you take your medicine?"

"Yes."

"You look a little feverish."

"Typical stuff. I'll be okay."

She sat straight and then moved to the edge of her seat. "Listen, I'll be here about nine to take you to the airport."

"Yes. Thanks. I'll be up early to pack. Thanks for everything."

"You're welcome. It was nice having you. The kids really enjoyed it."

"Well, I think you have a great class and they have a wonderful teacher. And thanks for spending so much time with me. You know, dinner, the picnic and everything."

"Sure."

"I loved your singing."

"Thanks," she replied, her eyes tender. "I loved the poem."

"And I will try to smile more."

"That would be good."

Chapter 6

The next day I returned to Philadelphia. As usual the dogs had heard my approach to the house and were assembled to watch me through the glass of the inner door. When I walked into the house, of course, they jumped at me, leaped upon me, licked me, gently bit me, and not so gently bit each other, in their ecstasy over my return. After receiving biscuit treats, they put on the clown or the gladiator and chased each other. When I took tea and fig bars out to the patio, Ragnar curled up beside my chair, Sono stood and pathetically stared into my face, and Tai Ping, in typical form, sprawled his seventy pounds across my lap and flopped his heavy, stone-hard head against my shoulder. For the rest of the weekend they would not leave me. I was not permitted to go to the drugstore for headache medicine or to the convenience store for milk, and on Sunday morning I was definitely not allowed to go to church.

It was good to get back to the studio. Even a week away from that room had enhanced my appreciation for the sheer sense of *place* it afforded. I knew I would never find a place so far from the negative, grasping hands of life. Of course, the serenity I found in it all was not because of the room itself, but because of the ideas I had formed there, the anxieties, the depression, I had survived there. No, it was not merely its physical peculiarities that made the studio my home, but the weird combination of its being at once a refuge and an arena.

Still, as I sat in the old painting chair and brushed pieces of broken charcoal from the easel's fixed palette I did not resist the power of the conglomerate odor of turpentine, linseed oil, damar varnish, gesso, wood, canvas, acrylic medium, and whatever, to remind me that, of all places I knew, this was where I belonged and where I wanted to be. From the cracked plaster walls to the splintered wood floors, the sweet rumple and grunge of everything welcomed me. Pushing from side to side in the swivel chair, I took in the drafts and unfinished pieces. A sense of purpose and joy came over me. Yes, it was very good to get back to the studio.

My return to the office on Monday was uneventful. Although the look from Sono, Tai Ping and Raggie was clearly pathetic as I walked out the door, it also said they understood the routine of my going to work on weekdays. It was a look that said they would be waiting for me to come home. As usual I caught the bus across from the reservoir and at Fern Rock took the Broad Street Line south. On the short walk to the medical school I thought of the dogs and, of course, of Judy. As I hadn't seen Brenda on the bus or subway, there would be little chance for our ways to cross until the end of the day. In fact, they had not crossed in months. One too many intense discussions had halted the charm and had led us, quite simply, to avoid each other. Rarely did my thoughts run in her direction. But they ran in Judy's direction often. In my office I started the water for tea and then opened my email, hoping for a message from Jacksonville.

I had been home nearly a month when I opened one such message to read, *The kids are all doing well. They loved your letters—thank you! And thank you for the painting set for Terri. No, it didn't bother her that it was used. I've decided to come to New Jersey next weekend. I'll rent a car at the Philly Airport and drive down to Cape May. I'll be staying at a favorite place across from the ocean. If you come down, we'll walk the beach.* When I responded with a positive, the plan was reconfigured so that she would pick me up at home and we would make the trip together.

My proposal to meet her at the airport was nixed by her insistence on meeting the dogs. Throughout the week I worried that this would not go well, and it was only as we crossed the Walt Whitman Bridge into New Jersey on our way to Cape May that I was able to relax and say, "I think my dogs liked you."

"I liked them. They're great dogs."

"Yeah. Thanks."

Then she observed, "You're worried."

"Yes," I replied. I knew the dogs were not happy to lose me again so soon. My justification was that they had done so well during my trip south and that the current fine weather would allow them to spend as much time outdoors as they wanted. They loved lounging in the backyard, chasing each other, and sleeping on the patio and under the bushes along the fence. Catherine would come over and feed them and let them in and out each day. Still, I was uneasy.

"The dogs?"

"They'll be okay, I think. It's great weather and they love their backyard."

"Their little part of the world, huh?"

"Yeah."

"Is that Tai Ping for real, or what?" she said to change the tone. "I mean, those teeth and jaws."

"I know. He's a bruiser," I replied, and when she deftly switched lanes, "Hey, you're a speedway lady, I think."

She grinned. "Don't forget, I used to live here. I know the roads." Then, dropping her speed a little, she added, "I don't want a ticket, though."

"Yeah. Not good."

"Did you bring your cane? I didn't see it."

"I did," I returned. "It's folded in my backpack."

"Do you take it to work?"

I sighed. "Same thing—folded in my backpack."

"I think you should use it more. You could fall."

"I don't need it that much. You know that. Besides, it slows me down."

"I looked online, and the blindness people say you should use it just about all the time."

"The ole template approach, huh?"

"It's smart."

"Everybody's different."

"And if you fell and really got hurt, what would your dogs do?"

I looked at her, then back at the highway before us. "That's a good point. I really don't know. I've thought a lot about it, though."

"You'd have to think less about it if you used the cane more."

"I know. And I'll have to use it more as the vision closes down. But for now, I'm okay. I don't use it in familiar places or when I have someone with me. Don't worry, I'll be careful. But thanks for thinking of the dogs."

"Tai Ping seems to like you a lot. They all do. You must be good to them."

"Yes. I think we all love each other."

She glanced over and then asked, "You think dogs can really love people or each other?"

I thought of how, earlier, Sono had watched me through the glass as I turned the key to lock the door, and of how Raggie, just behind her, had stared, just stared at me, and of how Tai Ping, sitting halfway up the stairs, had fixed his fiercely possessive eyes upon me, as if to remind me of his part in the claim on my soul. And I thought of how I had known they were still watching as we drove away. Finally, I said, "I think so."

"I mean, love's a pretty strong word."

"I know. You're right. But I mean it in a generic sense. You know, any strong affection, that kind of thing."

"Even so, where does instinct fit in?"

"Where does it fit in with people?"

"Why should animals even be expected to love?"

"They shouldn't be," I replied.

"I mean, the beauty of a dog is that it *doesn't* love, it doesn't have emotions, so you can count on it to act instinctively."

"Sort of like a gun trap with a brain."

"Very funny. Not very funny. Besides, I didn't mean that it should act with just intelligence. I meant that it should act *instinctively*—you know, the whole animal."

"Okay. A lithe, semi-intelligent gun trap with a keen sense of smell and hearing."

"Still not funny."

"Well, actually," I said, "I don't really consider them to be semi-intelligent. I was just being funny to make a point. Compared to a human's intelligence, of course, a dog's isn't even *semi*, it's much less. But that judgment is from a human perspective, and we have to be talking about the human sphere. In the canine world a dog is much more intelligent than a human. Humans have barely begun to understand a dog's intelligence in its own sphere. And there is irrefutable proof that a dog's intelligence isn't simply tied to its super-keen instinct. You know, dogs have found their way home from incredible distances, far beyond where any sense of hearing or smell or whatever could be effective. A dog's sense of navigation from great distances would make the best GPS look like a toy. And dogs know something of the psychic world too."

"And according to you, the spiritual world."

"You know, we're just talking about dogs, but most creatures in the animal world have absolutely uncanny powers. Humans don't know a lot about those powers, but the powers *are there*, they really are. You haven't watched many nature documentaries, have you?"

"Not many. Hardly any, actually."

"Well, when you do you'll see it's incredible what animals can do. Their powers of navigation and family distinction under impossible circumstances, and their powers of logic and strategy, are just not to be believed. And it's obvious that instinct or preprogramming of some kind or the great magnetic forces of the earth can't be enabling animals to act and think and achieve the way they do."

"Well, we want them to be useful."

"Do we, really? Why? Animals aren't slaves, they're fellow creatures, and they can be friends."

"You really sell your story, don't you? I just don't think you're being realistic. I'm sorry, but I don't. Humans are the masters. And if you don't want animals to be slaves, at least they're our subjects. They do what we want them to. You're giving them some noble purpose. You obviously know your facts about animals. But I just can't see this whole thing you have for them. It's almost mystical."

"I could never see them as tools. They are creatures as much as we are."

"Actually, I'm not sure I disagree with you, there. But there are levels of creatures. A canine isn't a human. A dog is just not a man. And I'm sorry, but this *love* thing is really far, just *far*."

I neither felt like replying nor felt that I was capable of replying, and for a few minutes we road in silence. Then I said, "Have you ever watched the clubbing of seals, baby seals?"

She sighed. "No, I haven't, and I don't want to, or to even hear about it, please."

"Well, let's just say, after watching it, I find it impossible to believe that humans are more noble than animals."

"You know what the realist would say, don't you? That seals just club other creatures, whatever they're going to eat. All animals do, that eat other animals. And clubbing is probably more humane than ripping them apart with your teeth or just swallowing them whole. It's all part of the balance of nature. Unless they're herbivores, they eat each other. And don't tell me about skins and furs. Please. Animals do stuff like that, they just don't moralize about it and feel guilty about it and brood about it."

Again we rode in silence. As I watched the highway's slipping under the front of our car and then imagined its passing away behind us I felt slow and stupid and somehow broken. And then I thought of Thor and the absolute look of incredulity in his eyes as I openly betrayed him and helped to shove him away from me and into the chamber.

"Could I ask you something?" she said suddenly.

"Yes."

"Why aren't you a vegetarian? It only makes sense that you would be."

"I guess, because it's natural not to be."

"You're not a vegetarian," she repeated, as if stating a fact in its generic simplicity.

"No, and my dogs aren't either. And I have great respect for them."

"Well, you did say *my* dogs."

"Yes. And they *are* mine. And I'm theirs."

She sighed. "You like nature, don't you?"

"Yes. I like being a cog in its machinery. I don't want to be the master of the engine."

"Yeah," she replied quietly. "Yeah, I got that. But you are passionate about it, *very* passionate, or at least you come across that way. You know, animal rights and all that baggage. Are you for animal rights?"

"Sure I am. But within reason. I'm for human rights, too."

"What about animal testing?"

"I . . . I don't really know. Basically I'm on the side of the animals. But if I had a child with leukemia it might be different. I mean, what are people supposed to do? If animal testing helps find a cure for disease, they go for it. And animal rights people don't have all the answers, either. They can't say where the cutoff is. The primate? The dog? The mouse? The microbe? It gets ridiculous after awhile, especially when most people believe, whether it's true or not, that animal testing speeds up finding a cure. So, I'm pretty heavily on the side of the animal, but I sympathize with the other side too. I guess, I wouldn't be much good to either side."

"What about animal testing for cosmetics."

"Well, there I think I'd side with the animals about a hundred percent. Except maybe where it applied to burns and disfigurement correction, that kind of thing."

"I had a fur once, a fox collar. Somebody said something to me, just a comment. I never wore it again. I kind of see their point."

"Oh, yeah, sure. I think the fur trade is basically criminal activity, whether the law says so or not. Again, though, I think using furs from animals that are primarily for food is okay. But I wouldn't argue. If people were really against it—just don't allow it at all. But I think the real issue is cruelty. I mean, the meat industry is a wretched world of cruelty. Everybody would say it, if they only knew. That should totally be controlled by laws written by animal rights people."

"So, you really know about all this stuff?"

I sighed. "Not really. I've read a few things, but I'm *so* ignorant. And I'm not political, I never was and never will be. I always sympathize with both sides. I'm no good at all. I'm useless. Neither side would want me. So, you haven't said what you think about animal rights."

"Well, I come down more on the side of people. Not for cosmetics and furs, I agree with you, there."

"Yeah, well, I don't think anybody's going to solve this stuff. Humans are too unidirectional in their thinking."

"So, you're not really political, at all, are you?"

"Not a whole lot. I'm an artist, what can I say?"

After a moment she said, "What if you lost the rest of your sight?"

"Probably, more like *when.*"

"Okay, *when.* Would you become political then?"

"What's the difference? Political people are fine. I like political people. I just happen to be an artist, that's all." When she didn't respond I sighed. "Look, I really don't know. I see what you're getting at, but I can't answer you. Maybe I would write, I don't know. For now, I paint, I take photographs."

Again the silence while the road passed under us and moved away from us, into the past.

Then I asked, "So, do you feel like you've come home again?"

"A little," she replied, happy for the lighter subject. "I've missed New Jersey, especially Cape May. It's kind of a life-line retreat, for me. And I've even missed Philadelphia. Going into the city had always been my cultural escape from New Jersey. But yeah, I've missed everything, and it *is* good to be home."

"That's funny," I replied. "I've been missing Jacksonville."

"Have you?"

I nodded. "Uh-huh. But you vacation here, you said. So, what's to miss for you?"

"I know. I think, just being here all the time, I really miss that. I guess I'm just indulging, being sentimental."

"Yeah, nostalgia's a pretty strong mode."

"I remember growing up here and how things were constantly changing. Some things stayed the same and were just part of your life. Other things changed and became more a part of your life. I remember Moorestown Mall being built and the housing developments going up everywhere. I remember when the Speed Line was put in, how we thought that was the greatest thing."

"I kind of had the same thoughts visiting Jacksonville and the school. It brought so much back to me. It was a real trip through the scrapbook, you know?"

"I know. But I think I could live just about anywhere. Could you?"

"With some exceptions, I think so."

"Well, our weather's supposed to be nice."

"Good." I reached to the back seat, pulled the D80 from my backpack, and checked its settings.

"You like technology." she said. "Computers, cameras, PDAs. I can tell."

"I suppose so." I looked at her top and skirt. "You don't, do you?"

"I like living things. Organic things. Life."

"Okay. But you and I met through technology. Email, airplanes, slide projectors."

"An old slide projector and an old screen."

"Hey, that was stone age. And I had to get those slides made. I could've just brought them down on a thumb drive. You *have* to upgrade."

"It was real."

"Come on. You know, a lot of the kids just went home and opened up their laptops."

"I know they did. But it was good for them to see the old equipment."

"Why?"

"It was closer to life."

I shook my head. "I suppose."

"I like to stay as close to living things as possible."

Rotating the lens ring fully in one direction and then fully back, I looked over to where her hair just touched her shoulder. I could almost feel her body under her clothes. All of this woman's body seemed so sensuously alive with life. I clicked the camera's power button on and off. Photography was marvelous. Matted and framed, hung in their wall spaces, photographs were beautiful, wonderful—wonderful but static. They could never pulsate with sensuous life. Making sure the power was off, I returned the camera to the backpack and closed the zipper.

After registering for our rooms we recrossed the tiny bridge over Cape May's tranquil harbor and parked for a late lunch. We placed our order for take-out and took an empty table on the crowded dock to wait. A light breeze from the water fluttered under our table's umbrella as we watched leisure boats crawl across our view.

"It's funny," she observed, "I've eaten here so many times and yet whenever I sit at one of these tables I seem to get a fresh dose of Cape May."

"Yeah, I know. You're right. It's an atmosphere that's always here. It's wonderful."

The flitting of waterside birds, the dieseled and gasolined odors from the harbor water, the sounds of people's shoes clumping upon the planks of the dock, all seemed to underscore our sentiments. When the number for our order was announced I didn't argue when she said she'd get it and watched her walk to the pick-up window and return with the tray.

"You know," she said as we ate, "Terri really liked the paint set. And your letter."

"Good."

"Why did you send so much? The canvas and everything?"

"It wasn't much. You know. The stuff sits around."

"Well, she loved it."

"I know. She wrote me a letter."

"She told me. She had me read it first."

"I don't know," I said, taking a drink of iced soda. "That's the way I started. My brother sent me an old paint set he'd bought years before to take an art class and subsequently hadn't used much. I remember opening the package when it came in the mail, and then lifting the lid of the paint box itself and finding the half-used tubes and stained brushes, the little bottles of turpentine and linseed oil. None of it seemed used at all, to me. It was kind of a magical moment in my life—I think, a moment I can now say was, somehow, pivotal. I had always done art. Charcoal, crayon, things like that. Actually, my brother had seen it, and that's why he sent the paint set, so I might try working in a more permanent medium. So, my painting really started right there, that was the door."

"Well, you encouraged Terri, inspired her, I think."

I shrugged.

"Don't you like inspiring people?"

"Not really."

"Why?"

"Fear."

She looked away momentarily. "When you inspire someone you just give them hope, right?"

"That's fair to say."

She sighed. "Well, I think it helped her, and I'm *glad* you gave her hope."

I shrugged again. "That was what you wanted, wasn't it?"

"Yes," she affirmed with finality. "And look at this beautiful weather. Isn't it gorgeous?"

I nodded. "Yeah. Yeah, it is."

"A little more conviction, please."

I chuckled. "Okay, it's *really* gorgeous." And then, inexplicably feeling mischievous, I said, "Watch this," and held up a French fry to the view of a seagull perched on a low roof edge not far from our table. Instantly the gull's wings spread and it dropped into a perfect glide toward my hand. As if it had done the trick a thousand times, the huge bird snatched mid-flight the offering with its beak and continued in its path out over the water.

"Good grief, they know you," she chortled. "How did you see that?"

"Oh, I see a lot. Should I hold up more? The others saw it—they always see everything. We should give them something."

"Stop. I'm not finished my lunch. This is ridiculous."

With the sun heading for home in a clear sky, we drove back to our rooms and changed for the beach. Wearing shirts over swimsuits, we took the outside stairs to the parking lot, crossed the street and the asphalt walkway, and stepped onto the sand.

"So, you won't need a cane out here," she said, adjusting her sunglasses.

I tugged at the bill of my cap. "No. Nothing to trip over and nowhere to fall. It's great."

The tide was out and the afternoon sand had been baked into a toasty carpet. At the water's foamy edge we turned south and walked toward the Point and the lighthouse. Except for making an occasional remark over the beauty or oddity of a retrieved shell or stone, or returning a polite hello to a stranger, we walked in silence. It was as if the sound of the collapsing waves of the mild surf was conversation enough. And it was enough. Everything was enough. The sufficiency of the sun, the sky, the sand, the ocean, was indisputably obvious. She was enough, I was enough, all of it was enough. And so we walked and listened and were.

When our hands touched as we stopped to observe a passing gull I asked, "Do lovers come here?"

"To Cape May? Well, maybe the older ones," she replied. "Otherwise, probably Atlantic City."

"We're a little out of the loop, huh?"

"Pretty much," she said smoothly.

"That's too bad. Or is it?"

She shook her head. "I don't know. But I could always drive us up to the casinos for a little glamour."

"We're doing okay on the glamour," I said. As we exchanged glances I could feel the power of her eyes through her dark lenses. And at that moment, it seemed to me that the surf was soundless.

Breathing deeply, she observed, "Nature is alluring, isn't it?"

"Yes." As I looked out to sea my memory furnished the sky and the ocean with blends of cerulean and ultramarine and the surf with nearly a rainbow's range of titaniums. Then suddenly, like one of the sea's dark surges, a sense of fatigue closed over me, and I said, "You know, um, I need to rest. Maybe now, I think."

She said, as if reminding herself of something, "Sure. Here's a dry spot."

I dropped to the sand heavily and then looked up at her. "Little rest," I said cheerfully. "You go ahead."

I watched her hesitate and then move slowly away and finally go and stand in a wave's receding water. I wanted to call her back. I wanted to have her come back and sit with me as I regained my strength. I didn't call to her, but watched her play in the froth of the repeating theater. Why should I interrupt something so splendid? Why should I be the agent of any interruption of her sense of life and beauty? I watched as she balanced on one foot, then the other, then ran for a short distance and ran back. She seemed wonderfully fitted with health and energy, as if she could easily have joined the sea gulls and played in the sky above me. Then I saw her look up and walk toward me. As she approached I looked down, as if to avoid looking at something fragile.

When she was close I looked up and said, "A mermaid."

She grinned down at me and tilting her head replied, "A sailor." Then with a serious tone she asked, "How're you doing?"

"A little tired. Tired and old."

"You look like you're in pretty good shape, to me."

"Huh. Very good. I used to be a bicyclist. I was strong. I'm not strong anymore."

She dropped beside me and patted my knee, her eyes on the horizon. "I know, I know. It's okay, it doesn't matter."

As a benign wave crumpled, sending its froth gently toward us, I reached for her hand. "You know," I remarked, "these jetties they've added are rather ugly. I liked it before."

"Yes, they are," she said, looking north along the beach and wrinkling her nose. "They've dulled the charm, I'd say."

"But we're sitting on a stable beach."

"Stability's good," she said. "But not without charm."

"Well, maybe a jewelry vendor or two could help bring some of it back."

With her free hand she pushed the glasses to the top of her head. Then she gave me a sly look. "And maybe a fresh artist could help, too."

"Oh, I don't know. They've probably got enough of those." And then I said frankly, "I think the vision's shutting down." And I thought of Thor, how I had betrayed him even as he lay beside the front steps, guarding my house. "You might have to settle for a blind man sitting beside your vending table."

"We'll need a bigger umbrella."

"I'll guard your jewelry so nobody steals it."

She laughed. "People don't steal in Cape May."

"I guess not. That's why we like it, right? Or is it the glamour?"

"No. We bring our own glamour. We're okay on that." And then she was thoughtful. "I don't know why I like it here. I just do. So, the vendor idea's viable, you think?"

"Seriously? Oh, sure. Why not? Do what you want. It's a great idea." When she didn't look at me but only watched the surf I said, "How about the other idea?"

"I think it would be charming. You could have your dark glasses and white cane, and I could have my sleek Italian sunglasses."

"That's one-upmanship."

"Just a little." And then she gave the sly look again. "Actually, I think I'm starting to find blind men attractive. Don't ask me why."

"Really?"

"Yeah. Must be my artistic side."

I nodded. "You know, I've always found blind women attractive."

"Attractive?"

"More like, erotic."

"Erotic? You paint pictures for people to see, and you find women who can't see erotic? Okay, the weirdness is back."

"Blind, thin, with tattoos—extremely erotic. I couldn't tell you why."

"Even before your vision loss?"

"Yep."

"Must be your artistic side."

"Could be."

"Or your weird side."

"You mean, like, dogs in church, and all that?"

She sighed. "Yeah, that's a little odd, I'd say. She pulled her hand from mine, hugged her knees, and looked farther out to sea. "Yeah, I think I'm going to get a lot of work out of you."

"Blind? With MS? I don't know."

"I do."

"I'm feeling kind of tired lately."

"You'll be just fine," she said. "You look in pretty good shape, to me."

"I might be able to weave a basket or two."

"Actually," she said, "I was thinking, more like, rugs."

"Rugs?"

"Yeah," she said, her eyes on the horizon. "You know, out of all the dog hair in your house."

"You noticed?"

"I did."

Then I asked, "So, do you think Cape May will want us?"

"I don't know," she replied. "I think the question is whether *we* will want us."

Beyond the surf an insignificant wave formed, like joy forms. It rose up gently, then collapsed and rolled in toward us, opening itself to us like a hand. Only she saw this process, but we both saw the joy.